THE QUIET OF SPRING

DARCI BALOGH

KNOWHERE MEDIA LLC

COPYRIGHT

DEDICATION

To my mother, who is convinced that I'm brilliant and probably understands this story better than anybody...

...and to the young man who changed how I feel about romance forever...you know who you are ;)

CHAPTER 1

*T*he science project was in danger of smashing to smithereens. It teetered precariously in the hands of nine year-old Randy Fischer as he made his way carefully down the driveway. It took all of his concentration to balance the colossal contraption, which to laymen's eyes appeared to be nothing more than piles of Popsicle sticks. They had been colored with magic markers, glued together and stuck onto a large Styrofoam base along with various other items such as wires, a tennis ball that had been cut in half, and what looked like an old bed spring.

While relatively light for its grand dimensions, it still blocked Randy's vision and made the trip to the black SUV that sat idling in the driveway more of a challenge than normal. Then there was the even bigger problem, Randy's five year-old little brother, Nicky, who was shouting–or "singing"–and running in circles around Randy.

"Mom, tell him to stop!" Randy yelled.

"Nicky, honey, would you please just get in the car?" Julia's voice came from somewhere on the other side of the

SUV where she was buckling nearly one-and-a-half-year-old little Sarah into her car seat.

"I'm practicing for the contest," Nicky responded, running and then cutting short directly in front of Randy. The science project loomed and swayed.

"Mom!" Randy shouted again.

Julia's face appeared above the roof of the car. Her straight, dark blonde hair was swept back in a fast pony tail, she wore no make up and she donned the classic stay-at-home Mom tank top and khaki shorts that all of the mothers seemed to wear the last few weeks of school. Even in this unkempt state of her morning routine Julia was still a beautiful woman.

Her shoulder length hair had loosened from the ponytail in places and pieces of it blew in the morning breeze, framing her face. Her eyes, hidden by sunglasses at the moment, were hazel and used to be one of her husband Jim's favorite things to complement. Her lips were full, nicely shaped and always quick with a generous smile.

At 38 years old and after three children she no longer had the slender figure of her youth. Instead she had full breasts and hips that sat rather well on her 5'8" frame, and a belly that rounded out instead of flat. She had heard that in France this type of belly was desirable on a woman, but she wasn't sure that was true here in America.

"Nicky, get in the car right now." Julia's exasperation came out in her tone. Nicky's rambunctious behavior always added an extra challenge to the most mundane daily activities.

Nicky stopped abruptly and looked at his mother, which allowed Randy to make a slow and careful break for the SUV. "What about the contest?" Nicky asked.

"What contest?" Julia awkwardly took the Styrofoam project and watched the boys pile into the car and click on their seat belts.

"Yeah, what contest you freak?" Randy was tired of rambunctious.

"Don't call your brother a freak." Julia told him as she placed the science project in his lap. Sarah, who was strapped into her car seat between her brothers, babbled with delight at the sight of the Popsicle sticks and immediately strained to reach them. Nicky was singing loudly again, oblivious to his mother's question. Since he was securely restrained in the back seat, Julia decided to drop it.

Watching for fingers and toes, she shut the back doors of the SUV and climbed in behind the wheel. Nicky sang louder and she could feel him kicking the back of her seat.

"Nicky, don't kick the seat. It's broken."

Nicky stopped singing but continued kicking, just a little bit softer than before.

"Can't Daddy fix it?" He asked.

"Daddy's on a work trip, " Julia answered with all of the lightness she could muster. She could still feel Nicky's Sketcher Hot Lights shoes in her back, "I said stop kicking the seat.

Nicky glowered at the back of Julia's head, but he held his feet still. "He's always on a work trip," he mumbled.

Julia sighed, pushed her foot on the brake and put the SUV into drive. Nicky was right, Jim was always on a work trip. The SUV moved towards the end of the driveway.

"Where's my potato?" Randy asked, a hint of panic in his voice. He was straining his neck to look at his science project from all angles and still keep it out of Sarah's reach. Sarah, unable to grasp the finger pinching bedspring, let out a small screech of frustration.

Julia stopped the car and looked in the rear-view mirror at her oldest son, "I don't know. Where is your potato?"

"I don't see my potato." Randy repeated, he nodded

towards an empty indentation in the middle of the multi-colored Popsicle mayhem. "It's supposed to be right there!"

Julia sighed, put the car back in park, got out, walked around to Randy's door and opened it, "What happened to it?"

"I don't know, Mom!" His voice held the slightest hint of contempt. Julia gave him a sharp look.

Nicky was still singing, his feet barely tapping the seat in front of him. Julia reached under Randy's feet and felt around blindly on the floor. "You had it when you walked out the door didn't you?"

Sarah, finally convinced that she was never going to actually touch the science project, began to wail. Nicky sang louder to drown out his little sister's crying.

"Nicky! Be quiet and help me look for the potato!" Julia scolded as she ran her fingers over a few empty juice boxes and along the crumbled remains of some teething crackers that were still on the floor of the car. Nicky abruptly stopped singing and held up the elusive potato where she and Randy could see it. Sarah spied the potato, choked back a few sobs and reached out her baby hand to grab it.

"What are you doing with my potato?" Randy shouted.

"I need it for my contest!" Nicky answered, indignant at Randy's tone. He adeptly kept Sarah's pudgy fingers from getting to the prized root vegetable. She stretched them wider apart and leaned as far over as she could in her car seat.

Julia, relieved at the sight of the lost piece of the project, leaned over Randy, "What contest, honey?" She plucked the potato from Nicky's hand and placed it safely back into it's indentation.

"The super hero contest. I'm going to have a potato laser!" Nicky answered. Sarah burst into tears.

"Freak." Randy muttered.

The living room was grey. The light coming through the windows was the clouded light of early spring, not the burning brightness of summer. Even though it was midday, 1:36 p.m. to be exact, when all of the inside lights were off the whole room just looked grey.

Julia lay flat on her back in the middle of the living room floor. She could feel the carpet prickling her bare legs making them feel slightly itchy. Her arms lay loosely on either side of her body. In her right hand she held her cell phone. The large bright numbers on the screen read "1:36".

This is the darkness of the day, Julia thought to herself. She said it out loud, "The darkness of the day." Her voice sounded strange in the quiet room. She looked at her phone again, 1:37. He hadn't called back yet. She'd called Chicago at 11:00 this morning. It was now two and a half hours later and he hadn't called her back.

When Sarah was a newborn and took naps during the day, Julia had often spent that time picking up toys, doing laundry and dishes, or cleaning ignored areas of the house. Everything had always been tidy and neat. Dinner was always on time. Kids were in bed by 8:30 every night.

Today, as Sarah took her nap upstairs, Julia's whole body felt heavy lying on the floor. It felt like she had somehow slipped between the earth and gravity, so that gravity's great invisible pressure was pushing her steadily into the grey, itchy carpet. She felt like she couldn't lift her legs if she'd wanted to–she didn't want to anyway.

She rolled her head to the side so that the carpet was now touching her ear. From this angle she had a clear view of what was underneath the couch. There were dust covered toys, socks, shoes, a sippy cup, and what appeared to be a hammer. She blinked a few times looking at the mess and wondered how the hammer had gotten there.

Her cell phone felt like a heavy stone in her hand. With great effort she lifted it to look at the time. It was 1:38.

Julia's arm dropped back to the floor. She let the cell phone slip out of her hand. She closed her eyes and felt the grey heaviness pressing down. Tears stung at the back of her throat. Julia focused her attention on inhaling a long, slow breath to keep from crying.

CHAPTER 2

The hall was crammed full of graduates, young men of all sizes and shapes, pushing their way back and forth in one giant mass of drunken (or near drunken) revelry. Their robes, which had been pressed and perfect earlier that day, now flapped open and hung loosely on their shoulders as they crowded around kegs of beer.

They chanted, laughed and toasted each other over and over again in the hall where beer wasn't allowed, lifting their plastic cups full of the foamy stuff high into the air. They let it slosh over the sides and land, unnoticed, on the top of their heads. The whole place smelled like beer and sweat and that particular odor that accompanies most rowdy sports events, mosh pits and riots.

Tyler Hughes made his way through the crowd towards Room E5, his dorm room. He was carrying a near empty cup. He hadn't drank the beer but had been jostled around so much on his journey through the mob that he was now wearing most of it as a pattern of wet stains on his shirt and gown.

Smiling at his college mates as he moved through them, it

was obvious that he wasn't really the party type. Some of them slapped him on the back or shoved him a little bit for fun. Others shot him comments like, "Aren't you gonna play for us, Zeppelin?" or "Where's your girlfriend, Ty? She bringing her whip?"

Good fun, the same kind of fun guys always had with each other, bordering on abuse. It was all in how they meant it and how you took it, Tyler knew that. In fact, today he didn't really mind at all. He was finally done. He was free. He was out of here.

Tyler at 6'2" with thick, dark brown hair that always looked like he had just rolled out of bed, wide-set brown eyes, a strong jaw and bright smile full of dimples was certainly good looking enough to be popular with college girls. He was also good-natured, smart, unassuming and could take a joke which made him popular with the guys as well. His main problem in fitting in during his Ivy League education had nothing to do with money–his parents had plenty, looks, intelligence or capability. The reason Tyler had never really fit in, and the reason he was so glad to escape it now, was that he had never wanted to be there in the first place.

He pushed his way through the door marked E5 and shut it behind him, drowning out some of the celebratory din from the hall. The room was small and empty but not terribly unpleasant. Most of his personal items had been packed into boxes already.

The window was tall and looked out across a courtyard full of perfectly groomed grass and flowers, winding walkways and ancient trees. His guitar leaned against the wall next to the window. Tyler tossed his empty cup into the trashcan next to the computer desk just as his pocket began vibrating, he'd set his phone to vibrate before the graduation ceremony. He fished it out and glanced at the name that popped up, Dad. He punched the Answer button.

"Dad!" Tyler covered his other ear with his hand to make sure he could hear.

"Son."

"Where are you?"

"Palm Springs. We missed our flight."

"Oh, I wondered what happened." Tyler sat down on his bed, which was now a bare mattress and box springs since he'd packed up all of his bedding.

"Your mother says she's sorry we missed the ceremony. She can't talk right now, she's having one of her migraines."

"Oh," Tyler felt the familiar sting of disappointment although, if truth be told, it wasn't completely unexpected.

"I spoke to Thomas Mathers." In his normal short-tempered manner, Frank Hughes had cut through any standard apologies or congratulations due his son and went directly to the most recent point of contention.

"Oh." Tyler could feel his father's disappointment through the phone.

"Tyler, he said you didn't show up for your interview." It wasn't a question, really, and Tyler didn't know how to answer so he remained silent. "Son, I had to pull a lot of strings to get you that interview."

"Yeah," Tyler felt himself backsliding into that awkward feeling of being a 12 year-old unable to explain himself. Damn, words always failed him when he spoke to his Dad. "Sorry, Dad, I had finals and stuff. I forgot to call him." He ran his free hand nervously through his hair, making it more of a mess than before.

"Stuff? Did you just say *stuff*?" Tyler could almost see his father's lips tightening, his jaw slightly twitching. There was a long pause then, "When are you moving out of there?"

Something he had a solid answer to. "Today. I'm actually

heading down to Austin for a little bit," there was no response on the line, "...with some guys."

"Austin?"

"Yeah, Austin. We're putting together some mu--"

"No. Tyler, you're going to New Jersey. Right away."

"New Jersey? Why?"

"Since you screwed up your internship with Mathers, you're going to do a colleague of mine a favor at his house in New Jersey."

"What? Dad --"

"Your mother and I are leaving for Milan and will be gone a month. It's going to take me a while to work out another interview for you." He sighed heavily, the weight of his son's future was taking up far too much of his time.

"Dad, I'm going to --"

"You're going to New Jersey. You're going to house sit for a very important colleague of mine. Do you understand?"

The door to room E5 swung open and a pretty, high maintenance blonde stood seductively in the doorway. Tawny Bryerson, Tyler's on-again off-again girlfriend–currently off–sported a graduation gown that matched his own except it was pristinely zipped up to her neck. Her cap was perfectly balanced in a coy position atop her well-groomed hair. The only thing about her that didn't appear upper crust were the black, vinyl stiletto heels that were strapped to her finely pedicured feet. She winked at Tyler as he stammered into his cell phone.

"I-I can't go to New Jersey, Dad. I've got some plans."

"To hell with your plans." The elder Hughes was done discussing it, the decision had already been made. "I'll email you the address. You're to be in New Jersey by Sunday morning. Is that clear?"

Tawny walked into the room, shutting and then locking the door behind her. A loud chorus of hoots and whistles followed her. Tyler shook his head "no", stood, and held up the palm of his hand towards her as if to fend off an attack. Tawny turned her mouth into a childlike pout and kept walking towards him, unzipping her gown as she moved.

"Tyler, answer me." Frank Hughes was not a man who waited for answers. Although he knew what he wanted to say to his father, Tyler couldn't form the words. He didn't know how to explain the trip to Austin, and Tawny's presence was more than distracting.

He couldn't pull his eyes away from her as she unzipped her gown further and further revealing skin and more skin until Tyler came to the conclusion that there was no dress. Instead of clothes as one might expect to find under a graduation gown, there were only perfectly tanned breasts, a smooth, flat stomach and a pristine bikini wax. When she finally pulled the gown off and let it fall to the floor he could see all she was wearing was a tight, leather belt with studs that was cinched up just above her hipbones. It looked more like a dog collar then a belt.

"Tyler!" The shout was in his ear.

"Yeah, Dad." He answered.

"By Sunday."

With a sinking feeling in his gut Tyler answered him quietly, "Okay."

"I'll be in touch." Frank Hughes hung up. As the call ended, Tawny reached Tyler's outstretched hand, grabbed hold of it and put his forefinger in her mouth.

"Stop it." Tyler said, pulling his hand away and wiping his finger on his pants. He clicked off the call on his phone and threw it on the bed, "Just, stop it."

"What's the matter, baby? Don't you want your graduation present?" Tawny, who possessed all of the pedigree necessary to be a debutant, looked more like a call girl at the moment.

It had been a long time since Tyler had enjoyed anything about her company besides sex. Even that had lost pretty much all appeal to him, with her anyway. In fact, he told her they were no longer an item almost a month ago. He planned to get out of school and be on his way to Austin. Tawny didn't fit into that plan at all, which had been fine by him. She obviously had her own ideas on the subject.

In this moment, even with her beautiful, naked body being offered up to him, he was so angry at his father for being the controlling prick that he was, and even more angry at himself for not standing up to him, Tyler felt a sudden revulsion towards Tawny, his parents, this school and his whole life rise up inside of him.

Tawny was set on her current plan and oblivious to anything else. She moved up close to him, pushed her breasts against his chest, and wrapped her fingers around the back of his neck, "Don't you want to know what I'm going to give you?"

"I said stop it." Tyler put his hands firmly on her shoulders and pushed her away. Tawny's sex kitten expression dissolved into one of disbelief and then rage.

"Are you kidding me?" Her voice rose in anger.

"Tawny, don't. I told you we're not doing this anymore."

"You're fucking kidding me. I'm offering you this," she twitched her hands up and down her naked pelvis, "and you tell me to stop?" She put her hands on her hips, looking a little bit like a dominatrix. Pointing at the locked door she asked him, "Do you know how many guys would love to fuck me right now?"

"That's real nice, really classy." Tyler responded. He hated it when she was angry, which was most of the time.

"Class? You don't know anything about class!" She swung a manicured hand at him and hit him hard in the chest.

"Put your gown on," Tyler was already angry, he didn't

need to lose his cool on his naked ex-girlfriend. He scooped up the gown from where she had dropped it on the floor and handed it to her, "and go."

Tawny's eyes flashed. She pursed her lips and snatched the gown from his hands. As she shoved her arms into the gown she spat comments at him. "You are such a loser. I came all the way over here and you can't even get it up, can you? I could tell, you know, I knew you were gay by the way you fuck."

Tyler stood as still as possible, not looking her directly in the eye. He just steadied his breath and tried to keep himself from boiling over. Jesus, it was like having to deal with a rabid Bobcat, he thought. If it wasn't so pathetically true, the whole situation would be laughable.

Tawny was fully clothed again, as fully clothed as when she had arrived at least. She stood proudly in her slightly disheveled cap, gown and stilettos and gave him a nasty look. He always found it amazing how ugly she could make her beautiful face appear when it was all twisted up like that. She unlocked the door and opened it, then with all of the grandness of a Duchess she said, "I'm telling your Dad," and walked out, slamming the door behind her.

CHAPTER 3

*J*ulia loved her house.

She, Jim and Randy had moved here when she was pregnant with Nicky and Jim had gotten his big promotion. It was new construction, not ancient like many of the lofty estates that were in their immediate area, but it had a beautiful old, lacy feel to it, almost like a Queen Anne style home. Not quite as elaborate or expensive as a real Queen Anne, Julia knew that, but it was still quite lovely.

Their home had two stories with giant bay windows on both levels, peaked gables and a wide front porch that wrapped around both the front and the West side of the house. It was painted white and had black shutters and black trim around the windows and windowpanes.

A huge back yard boasted not only a large deck for barbecuing that Jim built when they first moved in, but a swimming pool as well. Of course, almost everyone in this neighborhood had a pool. For Julia, who had grown up in a tiny, leaky house with not even a fence around the weedy back yard, having a pool of her own was something she'd never considered possible.

Nestled in between a few grand trees that had existed long before the house was built, their home had what realtor's called "curb appeal" and she felt warmed every time she arrived home, rain or shine.

With the deck, the pool, and the multiple flowering fruit trees and lilac bushes in full bloom, spring was one of her favorite times of the year. She spent a lot of time planting flowers and even had a small vegetable garden in a corner of the back yard.

All of her neighbors had gardeners to manage their yards, and Julia knew they probably thought she was crazy digging and weeding and watering all by herself. She wasn't the sort of person to have a gardener. It was a foreign idea to her to sit in her house drinking coffee and watch someone else take care of her yard through the window.

She took care of her pool, also. She could see that maybe doing the pool herself was pushing things a bit far. It was actually a lot of extra work, when you took into account raising three kids and keeping up on a big house, but Julia needed to feel useful. In fact, she could admit that her need to feel useful sometimes went beyond what might be considered normal.

Sometimes she got so busy keeping everything perfect that she felt almost manic. Cleaning every last spot in the kitchen, pulling every last weed in the yard and keeping three kids on a tight schedule was a lot, considering she also did all of the laundry, cooked healthy meals and provided a Norman Rockwell experience for her family as often as possible. The truth was she stayed up pretty late at night. Of course, that didn't really matter so much when Jim was gone. When he was home, though, it could put a damper on their sex life.

Today, however, he wasn't home. He wasn't getting home until tomorrow. So Julia had decided to take this Saturday and plant flowers in the hanging pots that she had for her front porch. The kids wanted to help.

"Mom!" Nicky was carrying a flat of fuchsia, purple and white petunias up the front steps, and he was losing control, "Help!" Julia left the low table where Randy was helping keep Sarah from pulling all of the petals off the flowers they were going to plant. She stabilized Nicky's flowers and walked alongside as he carried them proudly to the table, he grinned at her "We're going to have the best house on our street, Mom."

Julia smiled down at her kids. They loved this kind of project. It involved being outside, playing in the dirt and helping her complete a chore. She watched Randy take charge, as usual, and show his little brother and sister how to pull dirt from the bag and put it into the hanging basket. Sarah listened intently to her oldest brother with wide eyes. Nicky was impatient to try it himself.

She heard the familiar yapping of her next-door neighbor's Yorky-Chihuaha mix, and glanced up just in time to see the married couple returning from a run. Mr. Talvato was a short, balding man who was, she guessed, somewhere in his late 40's, and obviously wealthy. Julia surmised his wealth from a few facts she had noticed since they moved in next door. The neighborhood they lived in was pretty high end and the Talvato's house had to be one of the biggest and most beautifully landscaped in the whole area. They owned three cars between the two of them, one of which was a convertible Ferrari, and they held frequent elaborate parties around their pool during the summer that she knew must be expensive.

The single biggest fact about Mr. Talvato that made Julia positive he had a lot of money, however, was his very young, too tan, big-boobed wife. From Julia's brief interactions with Mrs. Talvato she knew that the young woman couldn't be more than 25 years old. What was her first name again? Julia tried to remember as she watched them stretch their hamstrings near their front porch. Mr. Talvato's short, hairy legs sticking out of his too big running shorts contrasted with the long, lean, perfectly shaped legs and tight little running shorts that what's-her-name was wearing. Actually, Julia thought to herself, they both look much too tan.

Just as she was wondering if it was a tanning booth or spray, Mr. Talvato caught her looking at them and shot his hand up in greeting. Julia nodded, smiled and waved back. Mrs. Talvato glanced at Julia but didn't wave. Instead she scooped up the tiny yapping dog and headed towards the house followed by her short, rich husband.

"Sarah, don't!" Nicky's voice brought her back to the task in front of her on the low table. Sarah had picked up two of the purple petunias by the top where the flower was, instead of the dark green, plastic pot that held them. "Mom, she's got them by their heads!" Nicky was reaching to save the petunias causing Sarah to screech at him in defiance.

"Here, let me see," Julia gently intervened and showed Sarah the right way to hold the flower. "There, now we'll get all this done then we'll take a picture to show Daddy." All three of their little faces lit up at the mention of Daddy and they set to work to make the most beautiful hanging baskets in the neighborhood.

The next afternoon Julia wiped off the kitchen table where she and the kids had just held a marathon Playdoh sculpt off. As she carefully removed all of the tiny, squished ovals of brightly colored bits from the surface of the rustic pine table, the kids raced around the house, preparing for Jim's arrival.

She was feeling the familiar blend of excitement and

anxiety that she'd been experiencing more and more over the past few years whenever he came home after a long absence. It was strange, really, to have such uncertainty when it came to your husband of over 13 years, but uncertain is definitely what she felt.

Things hadn't always been this way. She met Jim in college. He was one year older then her and just about to graduate. Her efforts at higher education were far less productive than his. She'd flipped back and forth between art classes and English classes, not always completing what she took on, and at the time they started dating she still had years to go before she could claim her degree.

That's why when Jim, a tall, handsome, driven business major who graduated and got a great job in another city right off the bat, asked her to come with him it didn't seem like such a great loss to leave college. She readily agreed and their relationship worked well for a long time. Julia dedicated her time to creating a great home while Jim dedicated himself to his work.

Lately the arrangement wasn't working as well for her as it had in the past. And she wasn't really sure why.

"Ma!" Sarah had toddled up to the kitchen table and held up a half crumpled piece of paper with various scribbles all over both sides for Julia to see.

Julia stopped scrubbing and took the paper admiringly, "How pretty!" Sarah grinned a semi-toothless grin at her mother.

"We're drawing these for Daddy!" Nicky proclaimed in a breathless voice as he ran into the room and shoved a slightly more recognizable picture into Julia's hand. It looked like a bubble shaped person with stick legs and something else that might have been wings sticking out of either side of him. "It's Daddy riding on an airplane."

Julia looked again and nodded with understanding, "Oh, yes. Very good, guys. Daddy will love them." Nicky beamed.

They all heard Randy slam the front door open from where he'd been keeping watch on the porch. "He's here! He's here!" Randy shouted. Chaos.

CHAPTER 4

$\mathcal{T}$yler stood under a towering portico that graced an equally towering front door on a three story high brick home. He noted the giant Grecian urns that flanked each side of the fine stone steps leading up to the front door. They overflowed with ivy and exotic looking flowers that he didn't know the names of, obviously the handiwork of a talented gardener.

He had already rung the doorbell of his father's friend's house and now rocked back and forth on his heels as he waited for Mr. Anthony Talvato to answer the door. He glanced around and noticed the house next door. It had a wraparound porch with hanging baskets full of petunias. He liked the lilac bushes in full bloom that lined the side of the house. There was something homey about a porch with lilacs and petunias. He was just catching the scent of lilacs drifting on a soft breeze when the giant front doors of the brick house swung halfway open.

A squinty eyed, balding man of low stature stood in the door. He looked Tyler up and down in a quick second and scowled. Tyler spoke up, "Mr. Talvato?"

"You Frank's boy?" Mr. Talvato asked sharply.

"Yes."

"What's his handicap?" Again, sharply.

"Excuse me?"

"What's your father's handicap?"

Tyler was slightly taken aback by the question, "Golf?"

"Of course, golf. What else?"

Recovering himself quickly, Tyler responded, "My father doesn't play golf. He says it's a waste of time."

At that Anthony Talvato smiled broadly, which made his squinty eyes seem even more so and revealed teeth so white they seemed to be glowing. He pulled the door open wide to make room for Tyler, "He's right you know, it's a damned waste of time." Mr. Talvato stuck his hand out and shook Tyler's quickly, "Anthony Talvato. Come in."

Tyler followed Mr. Talvato through a vast foyer that stretched the full three story height. There was a curved white staircase with a shiny black handrail that wound it's way along the wall and up to the third floor. Modern, smooth, white sculptures and abstract paintings of bright orange, deep purple and hot pink were placed strategically around the room.

The floor was white marble with black and gold accents. In the middle of the foyer floor there was a large motif of a gold and black star pattern, and on it sat a baby grand piano. To Tyler it looked more like an 80's rock star recording studio than a grand foyer in an upscale New Jersey neighborhood. To each his own, he thought to himself as they entered a large living area.

A small, grey and brown dog that looked like a Yorky Terrier, but bigger then any he'd ever seen before, skittered across the floor yapping like a maniac and lunged at Tyler's feet.

"No, Frasquito! Down." Mr. Talvalto spoke harshly to the

dog. The dog didn't listen. "Frasquito!" Mr. Talvato's face reddened as the dog continued its incessant yapping. "Kaitlyn! Get in here and get your goddamned dog!" Mr. Talvato shouted.

A gorgeous, busty brunette walked into the room. Her long, almost black hair was wet from the shower and she was wearing nothing but a fuzzy, pink bathrobe. It was one of those short numbers, Tyler was happy to notice, and hit her so high up on her long, tan legs that Tyler had a hard time not watching to see what he could see.

"Frrrrasquito!" Kaitlyn rolled the "r" in the little dog's name with skill. Tyler caught himself wondering briefly what else she did with her tongue, then abruptly turned his focus back to Mr. Talvato. He didn't want to openly leer at the man's daughter. Frasquito stopped barking and leapt onto the black leather couch next to Kaitlyn. She picked him up and adjusted the tiny purple bow on the top of his head. "Stop that," Kaitlyn spoke in baby talk to the dog and smacked him meanly on the nose, "Don't be mean to your babysitter."

"Babysitter?" Tyler asked. He wasn't sure he'd heard correctly.

"Yes, Hughes, we're not taking Frasquito to Turkey with us, I don't want his furry ass under foot while we're travelling. He'll be under your care, along with the house." He fixed himself a scotch on the rocks at a bar along the wall that was lit with neon pink fluorescent lights. He raised the bottle towards Tyler as if to ask him if he would like a drink. Tyler shook his head "no". "You have a problem with that, Hughes?" Talvato asked.

Tyler stumbled with his answer, "No, it's just...the dog doesn't really seem to like me." He reached his hand towards Frasquito to demonstrate. Frasquito growled from way down deep in his tiny belly and nipped at Tyler's outstretched hand.

"Nonsense. He'll get used to you." Mr. Talvato took a swig of scotch out of a crystal tumbler.

"Poor wittle baby." Kaitlyn snuggled the little dogs neck with her nose. He responded by wiggling his whole body and trying to escape her grasp.

"My wife thinks the dog will die of a broken heart." Mr. Talvato motioned towards Kaitlyn. Tyler looked for someone else coming in the room behind Kaitlyn. There was no one, and then he realized that the man was talking about the hot brunette in the pink bathrobe. Mr. Talvato kept talking, "I told her it's a goddamned dog. It will survive for three months. Longer than if it was going with us, because I'd probably kill the little shit."

"Isn't Daddy mean?" Kaitlyn said to the wiggling dog.

Wife. Tyler couldn't help but be a little impressed with the squinty-eyed Talvato's conquest. Well, he thought, to each his own.

CHAPTER 5

*J*im Fischer was hit with the full weight of his oldest son's body as Randy sprinted from the porch and leapt on his dad. A 40 year old, ex-football player who made sure to hit the gym even when he was on business trips, Jim was 6' tall and solidly built. Even still, the force of Randy's joyful attack almost knocked him over.

"Whoa, hey son!" Jim steadied himself and wrapped his arms around Randy's head and shoulders. Randy didn't answer, just continued his vice grip hug around his Dad's waist.

"Daddy's home! Daddy's home!" Jim could hear Nicky before he could see him. He heard the screen door opening and slamming, running footsteps, a crash of some kind and then Nicky came bolting towards he and Randy. "Daddy!" Jim stooped to catch Nicky as he took a flying leap towards his outstretched arm.

"Nicky!" Jim barely noticed the extra weight as he held his youngest son and felt his little arms wrap tightly around his neck, "How are you boy?" Nicky said something into Jim's neck that he couldn't understand. "Where are the girls?" Nicky kept his face buried in his father's shoulder, but stuck out his left arm and pointed towards the porch. "Well, come on then." Jim said as he half led, half carried his sons towards the front door of his home.

They reached the bottom of the front steps just as Julia was stepping out of the door holding a sniffling Sarah. Jim stopped at the sight of her. His heart skipped a beat, like it always did when he laid eyes on his wife after a long absence. She was so beautiful standing there with their daughter in her arms. Jim started to say something to her when Nicky turned towards his mother, "Daddy's home!"

Julia smiled at Nicky then at Jim, "Yes, he is isn't he?"

"Sarah fell down. Did you bring me anything, Daddy?" Nicky wanted to know.

Jim set Nicky down on the porch and unloosed himself from Randy's bear hug to walk up the steps, "She fell down? You okay my girl?" Jim spoke sweetly to Sarah as she shyly leaned into Julia and away from her Dad.

"Did you bring me anything, Daddy?" Nicky asked.

Randy smacked his little brother on the shoulder, "Shut up, freak."

Julia shook her head "no" at Randy as Jim reached out and slipped his arm around her waist. He kissed her on the cheek and took Sarah's tiny hand in his fingers, "How are my girls?"

"Daddy's home! Daddy's home!" Nicky did a spastic little jig in the middle of the porch and they all laughed.

She was avoiding him. It had been hours since he'd gotten home and after the initial frenzy of greeting the kids, wrestling with the boys, and patiently allowing Sarah to warm up to him again, Julia was giving off a stiff formality that Jim didn't quite understand.

He sat at the kitchen table, drinking a beer and watching Julia busy herself fixing dinner. He had offered to take everyone out, immediately read the negative reaction to this suggestion on his wife's face and changed his mind. She was probably right. Taking three little kids out to dinner wasn't always the most enjoyable way to spend an evening.

Still, Julia was exceptionally quiet, letting the kids talk and ask questions. She wasn't necessarily being cold towards him. There was something off, though, something he couldn't quite put his finger on.

Julia turned around as she patted a ball of hamburger into a flat circle, "Are you tired?"

"Tired?" Jim responded, "Not really. Not too bad." Julia smiled and turned back around. It wasn't really a lie. He wasn't physically tired, but after weeks of business meetings and sleeping in hotels he did feel a little dull.

His eyes wandered over the back of his wife and down to her full, round rump. He watched it rise and fall slightly as she moved back and forth putting the hamburgers into a frying pan on the stove. He felt heat rising in him as he thought about taking her upstairs to their bedroom. Maybe she wanted some alone time, maybe that would help her relax around him. Jim suddenly realized how much he wanted some time alone with his wife. He could picture pulling her shorts off and running his fingers underneath the lace on her panties, feeling her soft, soft skin.

"Dad!" Randy hurried into the kitchen interrupting Jim's daydream, "Do you want to see my report card?" Randy sat down next to his Dad at the kitchen table and handed him a sheet of paper.

"Sure, son." Jim turned his mind away from Julia and studied the report card. Nicky burst into the room waving his own sheet of paper and Sarah toddled after him clutching a worn out teddy bear.

"Daddy, look at my 'port card!" Nicky pushed his way in between Randy and Jim. Sarah tried to push her way between both of her brothers.

"Hold on," Jim said, "I'm looking at Randy's right now." Sarah, unable to make a space for herself at the table, started to cry.

"Oh, honey." Julia wiped her hands on a dishtowel and came to pick Sarah up.

"It's okay, sweetie." Jim said to Sarah as she cried into Julia's neck. He touched Sarah's back and then let his hand slide down Julia's side to rest on her waist. Julia moved away.

"Sarah doesn't have a 'port card." Nicky explained. Sarah wailed louder, a mix of sadness and anger. "She didn't have 'port card so she brought Bee-Bee Bear instead."

Jim smiled at the story and caught Julia smiling back at him. It would be fine. After the kids went to sleep he would take her upstairs to bed and everything would be back to normal.

CHAPTER 6

*J*ulia lay naked in bed, the white on white sheets and down comforter surrounded her with great wrinkly puffs and her head was nestled comfortably in her pillow. Jim's body, heavy and warm, pressed up against her own. He lay on his side with his left arm wrapped around her ribcage, just under her breasts. She listened as he snored softly.

The sun was coming up and the glow of the morning beginning to show through the bedroom windows. Julia touched the top of Jim's hand under the covers and ran her fingers along his arm. She pulled the covers off, exposing her breasts along with his arm. Without the covers she felt suddenly chilly. She pulled his warm, sleeping hand up to cover the top of her breasts.

The house was still quiet. She hadn't heard any of the muted thumping sounds that usually began when the kids woke up every morning. It was summer break now, which meant she could let them sleep.

Light was growing in the room and Julia turned her head to look at her husband's face. Half buried in his own pillow she studied the line of his jaw and the whiskers that had grown since yesterday. Jim was heavier then he used to be, thicker in his face and neck. His dark whiskers were sprinkled with grey here and there and his hairline was receding more then she knew he wanted to think about. She saw a patch of grey hair at his temple. That was new.

Julia turned her body towards Jim, and his arm automatically pulled her closer to him in his sleep. Every inch of her was touching every inch of him. The hair on his chest and stomach tickled her. The smell of his skin filled her. He smelled like sleep and cologne and the sex they had had last night. She reached up and traced the grey hair at his temple with her finger. She pushed herself against his stomach and could feel him start to rise against her leg.

A loud buzzing cut through the quiet morning light and Jim woke up with a start. He looked around, confused for a moment by his surroundings. The buzzing continued. Julia lifted herself up and reached over him to pick up his cell phone from the nightstand.

"Douglas is calling," she told him, "you should ignore him."

"Douglas, shit." Jim responded, taking the phone from her hand to answer it. His voice was rough from sleep as he spoke into it, "Yeah, what's up?" Julia nuzzled her mouth into his neck and ran her hands over his chest as he listened to Douglas. "No, that's not what I said," Julia felt a sudden heat between her legs as she tried to distract him from his phone call, "I...I think so. Miriam knows where it is. Oh, I see."

Julia heard a change in his voice. She looked at him as he spoke into the phone. He pulled away from her and sat up on the edge of the bed. "Okay, fine. Yeah, I'll be there." He ended the call and put his phone back on the nightstand.

"You'll be where?" Julia asked his back. Jim turned to her, a sheepish look on his face.

"The office."

"The office? When?"

"They need me in an hour."

"Now? You just got home yesterday afternoon!"

"I know. I know."

"You've been gone three weeks."

"They need me to be there when the New York guys get in. Miriam's on a flight, she won't get there in time." Julia rolled back onto her pillow and pulled the covers over her. She felt tight in the pit of her stomach. "Jules, I'll be back as soon as I can." He reached over and touched her hair then lunged at her quickly and kissed her on the cheek, "I've got to take a shower."

He jumped up and left her alone in bed. She could hear a muted thumping coming from the boy's room. The kids were awake.

Tyler shuffled across the cold tile floor of the Talvato's home in an early morning daze. His hair was askew in three different directions and he wore only a pair of blue plaid pajama pants hitched low on his hips.

The dog, Frankenstein, or whatever his name was, had been yipping for twenty minutes straight. The noise had finally infiltrated Tyler's dream and he had thought for a minute that there was a small, whiny fire alarm turning off and on in the hallway.

Now he was up and figured that the stupid dog was hungry. He scrubbed his face up and down with his hands as he wandered towards where he thought the kitchen might be. The little dog barked louder as he got closer which he took as a clue. It was like an inter-species game of hot and cold.

Tyler pushed open a door on his right to reveal a bathroom and realized he needed to take a piss. As he did (was it Frittata?) went ballistic in the hallway.

"Okay, hang on." Tyler leaned his left hand against the wall to keep steady as he yawned. "I can't remember your name." The little dog kept on barking. "It's Spanish," he said to himself as he flushed, "something in Spanish."

The kitchen turned out to be a giant room with a huge arched entryway about 15-feet down the hall from where he'd taken a pit stop. When he stepped through the archway the entire room lit up with motion-controlled lights and the tiny dog started springing high into the air and twisting his fat little body around with excitement. Tyler was fairly impressed with the display, even in his groggy state.

"Okay, okay...Frito, I'm gettin' it." Tyler opened and shut cupboards while the newly christened Frito zipped around his feet and leaped with joy knowing that his breakfast was so near. Tyler found a cupboard with a variety of what looked like midget tuna cans with pictures of tiny dogs on them. "Well, Frito, what's your poison? Savory Beef and Vegetable? BBQ Grilled Chicken? Turkey Chunks and Gravy? Eggs and Sausage flavored?" Frito growled, "Okay, Eggs and Sausage flavor it is."

Tyler located Frito's extra small purple dog dishes on the floor and emptied the can into one of them as the dog continued deep-belly growling at him. He even growled as he ate the food, so Tyler left him to find some coffee.

In a few minutes he discovered a cupboard supplied with a variety of single serve coffee pods. He couldn't help but smile at the similarity between them and the dog food. "What's my poison, you ask? Caramel Vanilla Cream? Island Coconut? Cinnamon Hazelnut Decaf?" Nobody answered him, of course, and Frito's growled response was muffled by the sound of his chewing.

The first official day of summer vacation was pretty gloomy as far as Julia was concerned. The kids had all woken up in time to watch Jim leave for work, which put both Randy and Nicky in a foul mood. She knew they had been hoping to do a Dad activity with him and now they were taking their disappointment out on each other. Sarah picked up on the negativity and spent all of breakfast refusing to eat and finally throwing her cereal on the floor, bowl and all.

Julia finally got everybody in line and they were now comfortably watching a movie together. This meant that she had approximately thirty minutes before one of them got bored and came looking for her again. She decided to take that thirty minutes and read by the pool with a cup of coffee.

There was only one book in the house that she hadn't already read. Her sister had sent it to her for Christmas. It was a murder mystery that wasn't too bad and she had read a few chapters right away before getting distracted by life and forgetting she owned the book. Now she would try to relax and read and, hopefully, Jim wouldn't be too late getting home. She donned an oversized New York Jets T-shirt and a pair of pink sweat shorts that she often used as pajamas and settled into a reclining patio chair by the pool, letting her legs warm in the sun.

Julia opened the book up to where she'd dog-eared the page back in January, sighed contentedly and began reading. Almost immediately a large, black spider scuttled quickly out from under the arm of her patio chair and onto her leg. Julia screamed involuntarily and, book in hand, leapt awkwardly from the chair, smacking at her leg and the fast moving spider simultaneously.

Finding herself standing, she checked her legs and arms quickly for the spider and when she didn't find it on her person began peering all over and around the patio chair. She finally moved the chair and forced the spider to make a break for it across the bricks. With one swift move and another quick scream Julia murdered the spider with her mystery book.

Randy opened the French doors that led from the kitchen to the back yard with a curious look on his face, "Mom? What's the matter?

Tyler stood outside the back door sipping his coffee from a gleaming white coffee mug. He had chosen Wolfgang Puck's Jamaica Me Crazy Medium Roast, black. It was already waking him up.

He surveyed the Talvato's oddly shaped swimming pool. It was an undetermined polygon shape, but looked a little bit like a giant origami bird, a chicken maybe. Three smaller polygon shapes lifted up and out of the larger pool at separate points. They were, he assumed, hot tubs.

Just as he was thinking that he might do a few laps when he was done with his coffee he heard a woman scream. It was coming from the yard next door, the lilac house he'd noticed yesterday. There was a pause and then another short scream.

Tyler put his coffee down on a small patio table nearby and walked over to the wooden privacy fence that separated the two yards. It was seven feet tall and stretched the length of the property. He stood still and listened, nothing.

There were some fruit trees in full spring bloom growing along the fence on the Talvato's side. They weren't more than fifteen feet high, but they would give him enough of a boost to see over the fence. He pulled himself up into the tree closest too him and found that he could peer through a sea of white petals into the back yard of the lilac house. From this vantage point, he could see most of the yard. It was very pretty, complete with a wide, wooden deck and a swimming pool shaped more like a pond than an origami chicken. The lilacs he had noticed yesterday at the front of the house continued in abundance in the back. They were covered with thick, fragrant flowers in all shades of purple and their delicious smell in the warm morning sun wafted up to Tyler in his perch.

Maybe it was the smell of the lilacs, or the ethereal look of the whole scene from where he sat surrounded by white blossoms and a few fat, buzzing bees, but Tyler believed that the woman he now saw standing in the back yard surrounded by three little kids was quite possibly the most beautiful woman he had ever seen. After noting immediately that she hadn't been attacked and didn't seem to be in any apparent danger, he had not been able to look away.

Her blondish hair was pulled up in some kind of tousled pony-tail, she wore a giant T-shirt and pink shorts that hung nicely on her curves, but it was her smile that kept his eyes riveted on her. She was showing the kids something on the ground while she smiled and laughed out loud. Spot on sexy.

Tyler felt his heart beating in his chest as he watched her move with natural grace around the patio. All three of the little kids followed her and all of them spoke excitedly over each other. There were two boys and a little girl who was barely walking. A few words popped out at him from the vibrant conversation, "spider", "book", "scared". The older boy said something that made her laugh even harder and she scooped up the baby in her arms.

Tyler suddenly realized that, considering there was no one being attacked, he was actually spying on this familial scene. He glanced down to find some footing in order to climb out of the tree when Frito caught sight of him from the back door of the house. He made a B-line towards Tyler, barking like a crazed, shrunken attack dog the whole way.

"No, Frito!" Tyler whispered harshly at the little dog then looked back at the woman and children.

The younger boy had apparently heard the ruckus and was now looking right at him. He lifted his arm and pointed at Tyler hidden in the fruit tree, "Peeping Tom! Peeping Tom!" The woman looked up with amusement and then some alarm when she made out Tyler's face amongst the white petals.

"No, no," Tyler said to them, he was suddenly acutely aware that he wasn't wearing a shirt, "Sorry, I just...I'm not peeping." The limb he was sitting on gave way right at that moment and he fell awkwardly to the ground with a loud snap.

Tyler lay sprawled on his back next to the broken tree limb, a wispy layer of white petals covered both him and the grass immediately around him. Frito continued barking, growling and making short rushing movements towards Tyler's ankles as he lay there, stunned. He saw the faces of two little boys and the woman pop up on their side of the fence looking down on him.

"Whoa, wipe out," the older boy laughed.

"Peeping Tom!" The little one again.

"No," Tyler refuted, "I'm not, really."

"Who are you?" Asked the older boy.

"Yes," the woman spoke finally, "Who are you?"

Tyler sat up, brushing petals off of his chest as he did, "I'm the dog sitter." Frito, taking advantage of Tyler's defenseless position, grabbed hold of the bottom of his pajama pants and began pulling them viciously. The woman smiled and Tyler felt his stomach do a somersault. He stood up to his full height and tried to look less foolish even though Frito still had hold of his pants. "I'm Tyler." He said, for there was nothing else he could think to say.

"I'm Nicky!" The younger boy practically shouted.

"Is that short for Nicholas?" Tyler asked.

"No, it's just Nicky."

"I'm Randy," said the older boy.

"Hi Randy," Tyler answered, then looked expectantly at the woman. His eyes locked to hers. He saw now close up that he had been correct in thinking she was beautiful. He smiled at her and she smiled back, he thought he caught the hint of a blush.

"That's Sarah, you can't see her cause she's so short," Nicky offered, "and Mommy."

Tyler raised his eyebrows, "Mommy?"

The woman was definitely blushing now, "Julia," she said, then busied herself looking anywhere but straight at him.

Tyler's smile widened, "Julia," he liked saying her name, "It's nice to meet you."

CHAPTER 7

*J*ulia didn't know why she didn't want him to touch her. He was her husband after all. This very morning she'd felt so disappointed that he left for work instead of staying in bed and making love to her.

Now, just hours later, as Jim handed her bags of Chinese food, a "peace offering" he'd told her over the phone, their arms and hands brushed against each other and she felt herself pull away. It was slight, almost imperceptible really, but it was there. She couldn't tell if Jim noticed so she carried on as if nothing happened, "How was your meeting?"

"It worked out well. It was a good thing I went in." Jim answered. The kids all gathered around the food as Julia spread it out on the dining room table.

"We had a peeping Tom!" Nicky told his father excitedly.

"What?" Jim looked to Julia for an explanation. She felt herself blush.

"He wasn't a peeping Tom," she explained.

"Who?" Jim asked.

"The Talvatos!" Nicky piped up.

"Anthony Talvato is a peeping Tom?" Jim looked both shocked and amused.

"It wasn't Mr. Talvato," Randy corrected his brother, "It was Tyler." Julia felt suddenly shy in front of her husband and concentrated on opening all of the take out boxes. Jim watched her with confusion.

"Mom killed a spider!" Nicky added as he took an egg roll and munched on the end.

"Whoa," Jim interrupted, "Your Mom doesn't kill spiders, and who is Tyler?"

Julia felt that she needed to take control of the situation. She took a deep breath and explained the details of her morning as she dipped chow mein noodles onto a Little Mermaid plate for Sarah, carefully avoiding Jim's gaze the whole time. Nicky re-enacted the smashing of the spider, Tyler's fall out of the tree, and Frito's attack.

It was all very entertaining and by the end of the story Jim was chuckling. Julia found herself laughing about it as well. Except when she laughed it came out too loud, like when she was forced to speak in front of a group of people and tried to crack a joke, or that time she'd drank too much wine at dinner following her uncle's funeral and had experienced tactless outbursts of merriment. Nobody else seemed to notice. Julia thought that a drink sounded pretty good right about now. She asked Jim if he wanted a beer and used it as an excuse to escape to the kitchen.

She made it as far as the stainless steel fridge before she had to stop. There, with her hand frozen on the door handle her mind was flooded with images of Tyler. The way he stood up and brushed himself off, the way his pants rested so low on his hips, his messy hair, and his eyes, the way his eyes had pulled her in when he smiled at her.

She felt a shuddering in her stomach she thought must be

visible to anyone watching. She opened her eyes, and only then realized that they had been closed. Her hand rested coolly on the door handle, not a tremble in sight. "What is the matter with me?" She wondered out loud. Nobody was there to hear.

CHAPTER 8

$\mathcal{T}$yler's feet fell rhythmically beneath him as he ran. Left then right then left then right again. The sound of the latest release from The Rocket Boys flowed into his ears through his earbuds, drowning out the sound of his feet landing on the road and his heavy breathing.

It was just after 9:00 am and he was excited to get a run in and get back to the house. He had decided since he was stuck there for months he might as well use the time wisely. He was going to get in prime shape, write some new songs, and get some play time in on both his guitar and the Talvato's piano.

Musically it had been a less than productive first few weeks. He had spent a lot of time sitting with his guitar on his knee, staring at the floor or the ceiling or out the window, one time he fell asleep. He hadn't written a note or felt inspired to write one. He felt brain dead. But today was different. He was going to put himself through a boot camp of sorts and by the time he got out of this place he'd be ready for Austin.

He was at the small park with the playground, which

meant he'd gone almost two miles. His plan was to loop around the park and head back to the house getting in almost four miles. A nice run if he did it every day.

Then he saw them. At the park he could see the two boys crawling on the jungle gym, a tiny little girl bobbling towards the swings, and Julia following close behind her pushing a stroller. He felt a surge of pleasure and only wondered for a moment whether or not he should stop and say something before he found himself turning on the path that went towards them and slowing down from a run to a jog. He would just say something casual and neighborly, so she didn't always think of him as the guy who was watching her over the fence.

He was watching her, however, as he jogged politely along the path towards the playground. He watched how she picked up Sarah and hugged and kissed her before she put her in the swing. He watched how she stood still for a moment listening to something Nicky was shouting from the jungle gym before she began carefully pushing Sarah. He noticed that she was wearing an army green tank top that fit her body closely showing the exact shape of her waist and her full breasts. He noticed that her hair had been braided into two braids that were pulled forward to rest on the skin right above her rounded chest. He noticed, suddenly, that she was looking at him.

Tyler slowed his jog to a walk and waved only a little awkwardly, he hoped.

"Hi, again," he said.

Julia smiled at him. Tyler couldn't help but smile back and he found himself kind of sauntering up to her, very much out of control of his own body language.

"Hi," Julia answered. She glanced down and smiled bashfully at the ground before looking back up at him with those eyes. Her eyes were a deep green today, probably reflecting some of the color of her shirt, and when they locked onto Tyler's he forgot what he was going to say.

He just stood there dumbly for a moment, and then, "Julia," slipped out of his mouth.

"Tyler," Julia responded. He nodded and they both laughed a little bit.

"You remembered." Tyler was pleased.

"I don't think I could have forgotten if I'd wanted to." Julia answered.

Tyler ran his hand nervously through his hair, "I guess it was pretty unforgettable, but maybe the embarrassment will fade with time."

Julia gave him a sympathetic laugh then noticed that Sarah was sitting patiently in the black bucket swing seat that had stopped swinging. She gave her a gentle push and kept talking to Tyler.

"Out running?"

"Yeah, yeah." Real smooth, Tyler thought to himself. He couldn't think of anything intelligent to say, but he didn't want to leave her presence just yet. Luckily, he was saved by Nicky spying him from the jungle gym and running through the thick sand to interrupt their little chat.

"Tyler!" Nicky was out of breath from exercise and excitement.

"Hey, Nickelodeon!" Tyler was relieved to have a less intimidating conversation buddy.

"What are you doing here?" Nicky asked as he climbed onto a swing next to his little sister, "Push me, Mom."

"Push me, Mom, what?" Julia reminded him.

"Please!" Nicky responded, Julia pushed his swing and then Sarah's again. "Where's Frito?" Nicky asked Tyler as he pumped his legs back and forth to go higher.

"I tried to bring him but he won't let me put his leash on," Tyler answered. This was true. He'd wrestled with Frito for ten minutes and nearly gotten nipped by him more than once before deciding to leave the little mutt behind.

"Lame dog-sitter," Randy said as he joined them, amused by Tyler's story.

"In my defense, I think he's a pretty lame dog."

"Can you do an underdog?" Nicky asked Tyler, "Mom won't do 'em."

"Sure," Tyler grabbed Nicky's swing with both hands and pulled him as far back as the swing would allow, letting the tension build as Nicky held fast to the chains at a 45-degree angle.

"Be careful," Julia warned as Tyler pushed Nicky and ran underneath him letting go at the last moment and sending the boy as high as the swing chain would allow. Nicky hooted in joy.

"Would you push me?" Randy asked, scrambling onto an empty swing nearby. Julia gave Randy a look. "Please?" The boy added.

Tyler happily obliged and they stood next to each other, he and Julia, for a good hour pushing the kids and making easier and easier conversation while Tyler forgot all about the rest of his run.

CHAPTER 9

*J*im had been home for two weeks and Julia had been distracted the entire time. She felt a twinge of guilt now as she sat on the bed watching him pull clothes out of the closet and carefully pack his suitcase. It was 5:20 am and the shuttle would be picking him up at 5:40 in order to get him to the airport in time to make his flight.

Julia got up with him when his alarm went off and made some coffee. His cup sat untouched on his nightstand next to his cell phone. She sipped hers while it was still hot. They were both too sleepy to speak much.

"Have you seen my dark red tie?" Jim asked her as he looked through a bunch of ties he held in his hand. Julia slipped out of bed and went into the walk-in closet, returning in a few moments with a dark red tie. "Thanks."

She sat back on the bed, covered herself with the still warm comforter, and went back to watching her husband. His big hands deftly tucked socks and ties that had been rolled into tight balls into the corners of his carry on bag. He would only take one carry on bag and a hanging bag onto the airplane. That would be enough clothes for five days even though he would be gone for three weeks. The hotel had a laundry service.

Julia drank her coffee and watched him bent over his suitcase, concentrating on its contents. She could see his shoulder muscles shifting underneath his blue dress shirt, and when he bent over a bit farther she could just barely see the spot on his head where his dark hair was thinning.

"Do you want me to make you some breakfast?" She asked him.

"Hmm?" Jim answered her absently as he studied the contents of his shaving kit.

"Breakfast, do you want me to make you some?"

Jim looked up at her, "Oh, no. No, honey, that's fine. I'll get something at the airport."

"You sure?"

"Yeah, don't worry about it," he went back to his packing. "What are you and the kids doing today?"

"I think we'll go to the beach."

"Oh, shit," he looked up at her again, disappointed, "I told the boys I would take them this week, didn't I?" Julia nodded. He started packing again, "Shit. Tell them we'll do it when I get back. Tell them I'm sorry, will you? When they wake up?" Julia nodded again. Jim shook his head and muttered to himself, "This merger is really screwing with things."

He didn't look up from his carry on to see Julia nodding in agreement.

It was stupid, she knew, stupid and juvenile and something she was apparently incapable of stopping. Julia felt like a teenager, or worse yet, a pre-teen junior high school girl standing in line to get a glimpse of Justin Bieber or some other ridiculous teenage heartthrob. Her palms were sweaty, her stomach full of butterflies, and she couldn't stop checking out the window every fifteen seconds–looking for Tyler.

Ever since he'd stopped to talk to her in the park she kept running into him completely by accident, a few times from her porch and more recently at the mailbox. At least, in the beginning it had been by accident.

In the few days following the park she noticed him leaving for his run at almost the same time every morning. Once her subconscious picked up on it there was no way of keeping herself from wandering outside at around that time, just to get a glimpse of him.

Her whole motivation, she told herself, had really just been to admire his physique from afar. Then he'd seen her and waved. Then she'd waved back. She felt drawn to him. It was like she was being pulled closer and closer to the Talvato's house every morning.

It didn't help that he was so damned friendly. The least he could do was to snub her or make her feel like the dowdy, old married lady that she was so that she could keep her distance. He didn't though. He was always nice, more than nice. He was warm and funny and she couldn't help but notice that he kept finding reasons to move in varying degrees closer to her yard as well.

Today she was packing for the beach. She'd been up before dawn getting Jim off to the airport and, in all truthfulness, she had been ready to leave a while ago. The kids were ready, the picnic was ready, and they only lacked loading the cooler and a few of the kid's beach toys into the back. So, why was she waiting? It was a Justin Bieber thing she guessed.

The kids were running throughout the house, decked out in their swimsuits. The boys snapped their towels at each other and it was getting to the point where she was going to have to get them in the car. She just wanted to see Tyler for a minute, a moment really. A quick interaction where he would smile at her with his deep brown eyes that twinkled when she smiled back, or maybe a short conversation where she could let his voice sink into her ears and slide down the back of her neck. Maybe he would make her laugh. It was an innocent crush, she told herself as she glanced out the window for the 100th time, just a little flirting to help her feel less down.

Just as she was thinking about giving up on him Tyler appeared on the front steps. Her breath stopped for a moment. Her heart flipped. Oh brother, Julia thought to herself, here we go. She didn't know how she got herself and the picnic basket outside so quickly. It seemed like mere moments before she was standing just a few feet away from him, her heart pounding, her palms sweaty. She had moved towards him so swiftly and he turned towards her so naturally that she had to stop herself short to keep from walking straight into his arms.

Tyler was dressed for a run. He wore dark blue running shorts and a faded grey T-shirt that had the word "Manhattan" written across the front. He looked comfortable and relaxed and incredibly sexy as he tilted his head and smiled at her, "Hi, Julia."

"Hi, off on your run?" She asked, rather stupidly. He nodded. Julia felt glued to the ground, as if she was connected to him by some invisible field of energy, and took comfort only in the fact that he didn't move either. She just stood there mutely for a moment, grasping the picnic basket.

"Here, let me help you with that." He leaned in front of her, so close that she could smell him. He smelled warm and spicy. His hand wrapped briefly around hers as he reached for the basket and his touch remained on her skin even after he pulled the basket away. She wondered how long she would continue to feel it.

"Thank you." Julia managed to say as she led him towards the back of the SUV.

"Going on a picnic?" Tyler asked as she found a place amongst the beach balls and towels in the back for the basket.

"Tyler! Tyler!" Nicky came racing around the back of the SUV, followed more carefully by Randy who was carrying Sarah, "We're going to the beach!"

"Hey Nicotine!" Tyler responded, "The beach? You going surfing?"

"Yes! No! I don't know!" Nicky leaped up and down as he turned in a circle, barely able to contain his excitement.

"Do you know how to surf?" Randy asked Tyler, a little impressed.

"Sure, I know all kinds of beach things."

"Oh yeah," Randy grinned, "like what?"

"I know how to surf, and find shells and sharks teeth."

Nicky stopped jumping, "Sharks teeth?" Sarah squealed with excitement as if she'd been waiting her whole life to find a shark's tooth. It was such a perfectly timed exclamation that they all looked at her and laughed.

"Mom, can Tyler come?" Nicky asked.

Julia flushed, "Oh, honey, I don't know..."

"He could help us find sharks teeth!" Nicky pleaded.

"Yeah!" Randy agreed.

Tyler looked a little embarrassed and Julia tried to save him from having to let the boys down, "I'm sure Tyler's busy, boys."

"No, not really." Tyler's answer surprised her but before she had a chance to say something Frito ran across the Talvato's front yard and into the bushes. "Damn," Tyler exclaimed, then quickly remembered the kids, "Sorry...I forgot to shut the back gate."

Frito tore around the front yard as if he was a toy that had been wound up too tight and let go, barking the entire time. Sarah pointed and laughed out loud.

"You have a crazy dog," Randy said as he put Sarah down next to him and held her hand. He called the dog, "Frito, come here, Frito."

"Oh, he doesn't–" Tyler started then stopped mid-sentence as Frito ran straight over to Randy and Sarah and started bouncing and barking joyfully around them. "He–uh–doesn't usually come when I call him."

Nicky knelt down next to Sarah and Frito rolled over in front of them to have his round belly rubbed. He looked up at Julia, "Can Frito come, too?"

"Of course they can come, but I'm sure Tyler has other things he'd rather do than come to the beach with us." Julia said with just a twinge of melancholy.

"I'd love to come," Tyler volunteered, "If it's not too much trouble for you." He smiled at Julia and her knees went a little weak.

"No, no, it's not any trouble. I just didn't think you'd want to come with us," she made a broad gesture encompassing her children and all of the beach paraphernalia.

"I'd love to come with you," Tyler stated again, more firmly this time. Julia could swear his voice was lower and softer, she was taken back for a moment by his steady gaze. Then he looked over at Frito who was basking in the adoration of the three little kids, "And it looks like Frito would too."

CHAPTER 10

*S*arah sat firmly in front of Julia on the purple and green blanket that was spread over the sand, flanked by a large red cooler on one corner and a pile of sandals and discarded clothing on the other corner. From this spot in the sand they had a fantastic view of the whole beach and the boys playing in the water.

Julia watched as Tyler picked Randy and Nicky up individually and tossed them into the rolling waves. He started off giving them a body surfing lesson, but that plan had quickly lost its steam and they were now joyfully wrestling in the water. Frito ran up and down where the waves licked the sand, barking continually.

Julia had managed to keep her cool during the ride here, but had experienced a moment when Tyler first took off his shirt after they arrived at the beach. Being so near his tousled hair, dimpled grin and bare skin had sent her into a slight dizzy spell. It was better now that he was farther away and she could watch him without worrying that he was reading her mind.

As she observed him splashing and laughing in the waves

with her sons she was glad he had come with them. It wasn't always easy to manage three kids by herself, and him occupying Nicky was worth the few extra sandwiches and potato chips he might eat.

And who was she kidding, really? It was nice to have him entertain the boys, but having the chance to sit back and watch him move, his back flexing as he hoisted Nicky high into the air, and his lean, hard stomach dipping in and out of the water, was invigorating to say the least.

Julia glanced up and down the beach. It wasn't too busy since it was a weekday. She saw other families and a few teenage girls tanning in their bikinis. They looked so young to her, but they were probably closer to Tyler's age than she was. It was likely that everyone there thought he was her son or maybe, if she was lucky, her nephew.

Julia sighed and helped Sarah get a juice box out of the cooler. Tyler had the boys walking along the beach staring at the sand now, probably looking for shark's teeth. She watched them for a minute and when she looked back saw that Sarah had been pulling grapes, packages of cookies and single serving potato chip bags out of the cooler and dropping them on the blanket next to her. Julia scooted over and set about reorganizing.

"That should keep them busy for a while." Julia started at the sound of Tyler's voice and turned to see him standing over her. His hair was still a little wet and sand stuck to his feet and ankles, but she felt the familiar drop in her stomach at having him so near. She looked past him to see the boys still scanning the sand for seashells.

"Did you find anything good?"

Tyler nodded and dropped down to his knees on the blanket, his thigh just barely touched her leg. He didn't move it. He held out his closed hand, palm up, towards Sarah, "I brought you something." Sarah got suddenly shy and turned to her Mom, burying her face in Julia's chest. Tyler was charmed, "How old is she?"

"She's 16 months." Julia stroked Sarah's hair and spoke softly to her, "Look, honey, Tyler brought you a present."

Tyler kept his hand in exactly the same spot, waiting for the toddler to respond. He had a natural instinct with kids, Julia had noticed, not too pushy, not too aloof. He began to open his fingers slowly and Sarah, intrigued, turned carefully back around to see what he was holding. There were three, beautiful white shells laying in his palm, and one shiny black sharks tooth.

"These," Tyler spoke in a whisper and pointed to the three white shells, "I found together. I think they're sisters." Sarah leaned closer to his hand, her eyes growing wider. "And this one," Tyler continued in a conspiratorial fashion, "is a shark's tooth."

"Dis?" Sarah whispered back at Tyler, placing her baby finger on his palm next to the white shells. His face broke into a huge smile at the sound of the little girl's whispered question.

"Those are the sisters," he answered, then gently moved Sarah's finger next to the shark's tooth, "This is the shark's tooth." He glanced up and winked at Julia. She blushed.

"Do you have brothers and sisters?" Julia asked him.

"No, I have little cousins."

"You're good with kids."

"I always wanted little brothers and sisters." Tyler said as he helped Sarah pick up one of the white shells she had accidentally dropped and placed it back in his hand. "My Mom says pregnancy is barbaric. It took her too long to get back into her bikini after I was born."

"Really? How..." Julia didn't know what to say.

"Vain?" Tyler offered.

Julia shrugged, "I guess it does ruin your figure."

"I don't know," Tyler's eyes twinkled as he looked Julia quickly up and down, "It doesn't seem to have ruined anything on you."

"Mom!" Nicky was running towards the blanket, "Can I have a juice?"

Julia was pleased and flustered by Tyler's remark as she reached into the cooler and handed Nicky a juice box.

"Not apple, Mom!"

"Oh, right." Julia took back his apple juice and handed him an orange juice. She looked back at Tyler who was watching her, it seemed, with pleasure. "He hates apple juice." Tyler nodded and smiled in response, but didn't say a word.

Later, they sat next to one another munching cookies and watching the kids put the finishing touches on a giant sand castle it had taken all of them two hours to build. Frito wandered happily around the base of the castle, guarding the children.

Tyler held out a cookie towards him, "Frito, come here." Frito immediately began growling and barking at him.

Julia smiled, "So, you're great with kids, not so good with dogs."

"Yeah, I always wanted a dog too, but not a scrub brush." Tyler put the whole cookie in his mouth. Frito growled again.

"You're gonna have to work on Frito." Julia broke off a piece of her cookie and held it close to the ground. Frito pranced up to her and delicately took the treat from her fingers.

"At least he hasn't attacked me since we got here." Tyler added, Julia laughed. He reached in front of her to get another cookie, his arm brushed across her swimsuit and lingered there for a brief moment. Then he broke off a piece of cookie and held it in his hand on the ground. "Watch this." He laid down and closed his eyes as if he was asleep.

Julia watched as Frito cautiously approached. Tyler opened one eye to see if he was making any progress. "Lay down next to me."

"Me?"

"He knows I'm faking, but he trusts you."

Julia did as he asked and lay next to him. She turned her head and looked at him, his eyes were closed. "What--"

"Shhh." He interrupted her. She giggled. "You have to be quiet." He whispered.

"Okay." She whispered back, feeling the urge to laugh out loud, she covered her mouth with her hand.

"Don't move," Tyler whispered and laid his free hand on her thigh as if to hold her still. She didn't move. Frito snuck closer and closer then snatched the cookie out of Tyler's hand. Tyler opened his eyes and found Julia watching him. "Success," he whispered.

"You seem to be wearing him down," she said.

"I do kind of grow on you after a while." His hand still rested on her thigh, she could feel the heat from it pulsing through her entire body.

CHAPTER 11

$\mathcal{T}$yler had been wandering, pacing really, through the giant rooms of the Talvato's house since he got home from the beach. He hadn't bothered to take a shower yet because he kind of liked the smell of the ocean that remained on him, and he thought he detected the slightest smell of her on his skin as well. He didn't feel like washing it off.

Tyler stopped at the living room window for the 100th time since he'd walked in the door near dusk. From this spot he could see a section of Julia's house and front porch, the windows glowed with orange light. He stood in the dark partly because he didn't care to turn on all of the lights and partly because he knew that if he did she would be more likely to see him standing there, staring at her house.

"Jesus," he said to himself, and ran his hand through his hair. Images of her laughing in the sun, leaning so close to him with Sarah to look at the shells in his hand, and laying next to him on the blanket were rocketing through his mind. He shook his head as if to erase them.

He turned abruptly and went upstairs towards the music

room. Maybe he should focus on playing for a while. He needed to get in some practice today anyway. His cell phone beeped at him from his pocket. He took it out with half of a hope that it was Julia. He looked down at the name and sighed, then hit the button to answer.

"Dad."

"Tyler, have you lost your mind?"

"What?"

"Have you lost your mind?"

Tyler stopped in the middle of the hallway and took a deep breath, "Dad, what are you talking about?"

"I just got off the phone with Tawny Bryerson, and she informed me that you two are no longer dating." Tyler didn't know what to say. "Is that true?"

"Yes, Dad, that's correct." Tyler knew that the significant pause following this statement was because his father had to take a few deep breaths to keep calm.

Finally Frank Hughes spoke, "It's like you don't have any sense at all. Do you have any idea who Daniel Bryerson is? Do you have any concept of who that man knows?"

"Yes, Dad, I guess--"

"You guess?" Another pause, "Tawny told me that you broke up with her? Is that correct?"

"Yes, I did. She's a little overbearing." In fact, he'd blocked her number from his phone a few weeks ago to end the nasty texts and messages that she'd been leaving.

"You're not gay are you?"

"What?"

"You heard me."

"No, Dad, I can't believe we're even talking about this. I don't like her, that's all."

"Tyler, I'm going to tell you this once more and hope it finally sinks into your thick skull. If you want to get anywhere in life you're going to have to learn to swallow some of this dreamy, emotional bullshit and make a few strategic decisions." Tyler listened silently. "I suggest you get on the phone right now and do some backstroking with that little girl. I don't care if she's a crazy bitch from hell, you need her connections, do you understand?"

"Dad, I--"

"I'm not listening to any more bullshit. We have a dinner reservation. Do what I say." And with that he was gone.

The next morning, after a restless night of not sleeping, Tyler laid on a lounge chair next to the origami pool. His guitar rested on its own lounge chair next to him, a cup of coffee sat on the ground within arms reach. He had come outside intending to practice guitar and, hopefully, wake up a little before going on his jog. However, the sunshine warmed him and he realized how tired he was from his sleepless night. So he stretched out for a minute and closed his eyes. That had been a while ago, and he was still resting, only disturbed every now and then by the clicking of Frito's nails on the tile next to the pool.

Something small dropped on his leg, it felt like a little rock. Tyler opened one eye and checked it out. There was a tiny, green pod on the tile next to him. It must have fallen from a tree. He closed his eyes again and another green pod hit his stomach. He heard snickering from the other side of the fence in Julia's yard, and kept his eyes closed, waiting.

Another green pod landed on his cheek and, without opening his eyes, Tyler spoke, "Yo, Nick-Knack, what are you doing?" More snickering and then muffled voices talking. There was a pause and some rustling around and suddenly Tyler was being pelted with dozens of little green pods all at once. He leaped up off of the lounge chair causing a wild yipping response from Frito, and ran as fast as he could towards the fence where he saw Nicky and Randy's heads popped over the top. They shouted with excitement and disappeared from view.

Tyler clambered up the fruit tree near the fence and peered over to find Randy and Nicky watching for him. They had that particular look of wild glee on their faces that little boys get when they chase each other for fun. Tyler gave them a nod, "What are you boys up to?"

"Nothing," Randy answered, mimicking Tyler's cool response.

Nicky, on the other hand, began jumping in a circle with excitement, "You're gonna fall on your butt again!" He shouted. This sent both of the boys into peals of laughter.

Tyler grinned and shook his head as the boys laughed it out. He glanced around the rest of the yard, no sign of Julia as far as he could see, "Where's your Mom?"

"She's making pancakes," Randy answered, "Hey, do you really play the guitar?"

Tyler nodded, "Yep."

"Would you teach me?" Randy asked, more serious now than before.

"Sure."

"Wanna come over and have pancakes?" Nicky asked.

Yes, Tyler thought to himself, I really do. "Pancakes?"

"Come over! Mom's making tons of chocolate chip pancakes!" Nicky urged.

"I don't know, maybe you should ask her first." Tyler didn't know if he should pursue the pancake thing too readily. How would it look to Julia?

"She wants you to come." Nicky said. He had picked up a random stick and was digging it into the grass.

"She said so?" Tyler asked.

Nicky shook his head, "No, but she laughs more when you're with us."

"I'll go ask if it's okay," Randy offered and took off before Tyler could think of what to say.

Within a few minutes Tyler was ushered into Julia's kitchen by Nicky. Julia wore men's boxer shorts and an ECKO T-shirt that had been cut across the top and on the sleeves, obviously her pajamas.

"He's here!" Nicky announced.

"Good morning," Tyler said.

Julia smiled at him and nervously pushed her still messy hair back from her face, "Hi, sorry, I'm not really dressed yet."

"No, I'm sorry. I didn't mean to intrude." Tyler secretly loved the fact that she wasn't dressed yet. "It's just they said I might be able to mooch some chocolate chip pancakes from you."

"You're not intruding," Julia answered sweetly, "Have a seat." She motioned to the kitchen table.

"You sure you have enough?" Tyler asked.

"Oh, yes. I always make too many anyway."

Tyler sat down at the table and watched Julia pour pancake batter in four small circles onto a large griddle then sprinkle a few chocolate chips over the top of each.

"Do you want some coffee?" She asked and started towards the coffee pot on the counter.

"Here, let me." Tyler stood up and moved next to her. He laid his hand on her arm to keep her where she was. Her skin was so soft. "Where are your cups? I can get it."

"There." She pointed to a cupboard door and went quickly back to flip the pancakes.

Tyler poured his coffee and saw a mug sitting on the counter near the stove, "Want me to warm you up?"

"What?" Julia turned to look at him.

"Your coffee," Tyler motioned towards her half full cup, "Want me to warm you up?"

She blushed and nodded, turning back to the business of pancakes, "Yes, thanks."

As she cooked Tyler leaned against the counter just a few feet behind her, watching her pour batter, sprinkle chips, flip pancakes, and—his personal favorite—open the oven door and bend over to place fresh pancakes on the growing stack inside.

He loved how her hair fell so disorderly down her back and around her neck. He loved how she looked so warm and rumpled. He wanted to run his hand down her back and slide it over the soft flannel of her boxer shorts.

The kids ran in and out in varying degrees of disruption as Julia cooked. She managed to keep making pancakes, which filled the room with the delicious scent of a home-made breakfast. All the while she made friendly conversation with Tyler about a wide variety of subjects that he couldn't remember later that day when he was alone again.

What he did remember was her voice, so engaging when she was telling a funny story, so tender when she talked to her kids. The way she smiled at him over a stack of syrupy pancakes and steaming mugs of coffee, the way the light that streamed in through the window seemed to give her a halo, and the way her eyes shone.

They talked at her kitchen table all morning. It must have been hours, but it didn't feel very long to him. One time when she was helping Sarah get more milk in her sippy cup he sat back, looked around and wondered what it would be like to have something like this every day, so easy, so welcoming, so...nice. That word didn't exactly convey what he felt, but he couldn't think of another one.

More than once during their morning chat he found himself reaching for her, touching her arm or her hand while he spoke. He noticed that he was leaning towards her over the table, and that she was leaning towards him. Their knees touched, their arms brushed against one another, he felt close enough to her to consider brushing a tendril of hair from her cheek, but stopped himself just in time.

Finally, Tyler decided that he should excuse himself and go home before he outstayed his welcome. He said as much, and Julia assured him that she hadn't minded at all. "In fact," she revealed, "It was fun to have you here." With that Tyler made his way towards the door and was ninja attacked by Nicky.

"Nicky," Julia scolded him, "Tyler needs to go home now, he has things to do."

"No, he doesn't." Nicky continued to ninja kick at Tyler as Tyler deftly picked him up, carried him sideways to the couch, and plopped him down. "He doesn't have a job!"

"True." Tyler agreed.

"Hey, Tyler." Randy called to him from upstairs.

"Yeah?"

"Can I come over and you can teach me the guitar?"

"Sure, buddy, any time." Tyler held his hand out to Sarah for a high-five, which she gave him. Then he winked at Julia and opened the door to leave.

"Tyler," Nicky shouted from the couch.

"Yeah?"

"Do you want to come to my birthday party?" Tyler looked at Julia for explanation.

"Oh, honey," she said to Nicky, "It's a little kid's birthday party. I don't think Tyler wants to come."

"Other grown ups are coming! Grandma and Grandpa are coming! And he can bring Frito!" Nicky answered, "Can Frito do any tricks?"

Tyler thought about it, "I don't know. Maybe we could teach him something. When's the party?"

"Saturday!" Nicky said eagerly.

Tyler looked to Julia for permission, which she granted with a quick nod. He grinned. "All right, Saturday it is."

"Whoopee!" Nicky cried out as he bounced himself onto the floor.

Whoopee doesn't quite cover it, Tyler thought to himself as he shut the door behind him.

CHAPTER 12

*J*im looked out the window of his Chicago office at the street traffic below. He had just ushered the last of his clients out of his final meeting of the day and needed to take a few moments to decompress. In a minute he would buzz his secretary and have her join him and go over his schedule for tomorrow, but for now he just wanted to stand quietly and watch the cars ebbing and flowing.

He'd learned a long time ago how important decompression was for him. He had to do it at work and at home in order to function. Of course, at work it was easier.

It's not that he didn't like being at home, but three kids could create quite an uproar. Two kids had been manageable, but only barely with Nicky's excitable personality. Sometimes Jim wondered if he didn't have ADD or ADHD or whatever it was that kids had when they couldn't sit still. Julia refused to label him at such a young age, insisting that he was just energetic and as long as they paid attention and kept him occupied he would be fine. Anyway, all thought of relaxing at home had disappeared when Sarah was born.

Jim went back to his desk and picked up one of the three framed pictures of his family that were proudly displayed there for all to see. It was the one where they'd all been in the swimming pool, Sarah couldn't have been more than six months old. Julia's sister, Maggie, had been visiting. She's the one that had snapped the photo. It was a good picture.

Maggie was a photographer and she had this great way of capturing the essence of a moment like nobody else seemed to be able to do. She'd sent this to him for Christmas, framed and ready to sit on his desk. All five of them were frozen in time, goofing off in the pool, smiling and waving for the camera. The frame had the words "Moments to Remember" written in block letters along the bottom.

Jim smiled and picked up his cell phone. He checked the most recent calls, none of them from Julia. He sat down as he called her. He had a sudden urge to know what they'd been doing all day, and to hear Sarah's babble as she tried to have a conversation with him over the phone.

There was no answer and within a few rings Julia's recorded voice asked him to leave a message. Jim leaned back in his black leather, swivel chair. "Hey, Babe, just taking a break and seeing what you're up to today. Oh, and I got my flight info back for Friday. I'll be home around seven. Do you want me to get anything for Nicky's birthday while I'm in the big city? Think about it. Love you." He hung up.

With that Jim laid his phone back on his desk and hit the intercom button on the sleek, black desk phone, "Christine?"

"Yes?" Christine answered.

"Can you come in here for a minute and bring tomorrow's schedule."

"Sure."

"Thanks." Jim swiveled his chair back around to look out the window while he waited. The light outside was gradually changing into the glow of late afternoon.

CHAPTER 13

*J*ulia felt like she was tipsy. She'd been overly happy and prone to giggling all morning as she got the house ready for Nicky's party. She found herself spontaneously playing around with the kids and able to enjoy Nicky's excitement instead of feeling like it was wearing on her nerves. She'd even been flirting with Jim a little bit. About mid-morning the realization washed over her that she couldn't remember the last time she'd felt this happy. This epiphany immediately gave way to shame because Julia knew, deep down, that it was all due to Tyler's impending arrival.

Fortunately her family, including Jim, were completely unaware of Tyler's affect on her mood and they simply enjoyed her and the party preparations. Julia had decided to go with it and allow herself a tiny bit of titillation, seeing as it was uplifting her entire family and Nicky's birthday experience. Maybe that was bad, she wasn't sure, but it was the only way she could manage the situation.

Kids and parents arrived to find the entire back yard pool area decked out in Pirates of the Caribbean decor. And

Nicky, complete with plastic sword and eye patch, was in full pirate mode.

Jim's parents had come down for the occasion. Ed and Tracy lived just forty-five minutes away, so they were usually able to make it to big occasions. Every now and then they would take the kids for an overnight at their place to "give Julia a break". Julia didn't think Tracy could handle Nicky's over the top personality very well, and felt that her mother-in-law held her personally responsible for the way that he acted. Her intimation was that Julia obviously needed a break from parenting since she was doing such a poor job of it. Even though she didn't always feel comfortable with Jim's parents, today she was in high spirits and nothing seemed to be able to get her down, especially after Tyler arrived.

He showed up with Frito, who was donning a tiny, red bandana around his neck, in honor of the pirate theme. Tyler wore cargo shorts and a white T-shirt, but with his tan and his thick, dark hair, he looked like he'd just walked out of a magazine ad for Tall, Dark & Handsome. Jim had been on the phone in his home office when Tyler arrived and missed the fuss that Frito's arrival caused with the children, and Tyler's arrival caused with the other mothers.

Tyler helped Nicky show off the tricks that they had taught Frito over the last few days. All of the children stood around admiring the little dog, while their moms admired Tyler. The women giggled and nudged each other every time they had a chance, and Felicia, little Brandon's mom, flirted with him shamelessly, even reaching out and squeezing his biceps a few times.

Julia felt a little proud, a little jealous and more than a little nervous as she stood back and observed the actions of the other women. None of them were really close friends of hers, more acquaintances, but she suddenly wondered if she had been acting as ridiculous over Tyler as this group of 40-

THE QUIET OF SPRING

ish women were acting now. More than that, she worried that perhaps Jim could read her emotions just as easily when he got off of his business call.

Julia decided that the best course of action was to ignore Tyler for the duration of the party. She didn't want the other mothers, or Jim's parents, or Jim especially to suspect that she had anything other than neighborly feelings for their young house sitting friend.

It wasn't hard to find things to do that kept her away from Tyler, but it was impossible for her to ignore him. His presence in her back yard drew her towards him, even when she was dedicating herself to a task somewhere else. She was constantly noticing him, seeing him out of the corner of her eye, hearing him laughing and talking, pausing to watch him play with Nicky and the other boys, turning to find him standing so near her that on a few occasions their bodies brushed together.

On one of those occasions Julia was busily collecting discarded napkins off of the food table when she turned around and bumped right into Tyler, spilling some of the beer he was holding in a Jack Sparrow cup. He deftly held the cup up and away from the both of them and steadied her with his other hand, "Whoa."

"Jules!" It was Jim. "Careful. You okay?" Jim had been standing on the other side of Tyler engrossed in a conversation with the young man about Top 100 Ivy League colleges. Julia stopped short and blushed madly, she couldn't tell if Jim was inquiring after her well-being or Tyler's.

Tyler continued holding her arm and she felt the now familiar response of tingling heat that seemed to move from his hand, through her bare skin and into her bloodstream. She stammered the beginning of a response when Jim's cell phone rang and he pulled it out of his pocket.

"Hold on," Jim said as he looked at the number then

groaned, "I've got to take this. I'll be inside." And with that he was gone, leaving Tyler holding Julia's arm.

A full range of emotions washed through her in a few, short moments. She was both angry and embarrassed, and something else. She felt a tremor move through her body. Tyler watched her steadily, never releasing her arm. Suddenly, hot tears welled up in her eyes and she blinked them back quickly before returning his gaze. She couldn't think of what to say or what to do.

"Let me help you," He said quietly as he slid his hand down her arm to her hands and took the wad of crumpled napkins that she was holding tightly. She nodded and then turned and walked quickly into the kitchen with Tyler following close on her heels.

Her kitchen, normally so welcoming and bright, seemed claustrophobic and much, much too hot. She couldn't breathe it was so hot. Julia leaned her hands on the counter and took a few shallow breaths. Tyler put down his cup and the napkins and placed a strong, supportive hand on her lower back, "Julia, what's wrong?"

"I just -- it's just --" Julia put her hands over her face as the tears would no longer be held back. She cried silently for only a few moments before Tyler turned her towards him and wrapped his arms around her, pulling her into his chest.

She was surprised at how quickly she responded to his touch, moving her hands away from her face, over his broad shoulders and around his neck. The wonderful tingly heat that his touch brought to her skin now covered her entire body and she couldn't keep herself from pressing her cheek, and nearly her mouth, against his neck.

Tyler bent his cheek into her hair. He pulled her even closer to him so that her breasts and stomach were firm against his body. Her body seemed to come alive under his touch and Julia, without thinking, let her hands caress his shoulders and move up the back of his neck into his hair. He inhaled sharply and let one of his hands slip just below her lower back.

She wanted his hands to keep moving lower and lower until he was holding her behind in his strong grip and then lift her up onto the kitchen counter. She wanted to wrap her legs around his waist from her perch on the counter, take off his white T-shirt and move her open mouth over every inch of his neck and his chest, tasting his skin. She wanted Tyler to pull her shirt open and off of her shoulders, then feel his fingers unclasp her bra. She wanted to watch his eyes take in her full, naked breasts and then press them against him as he held her and kissed her mouth deeply, right there in her own kitchen.

She wanted all of this so badly, so Julia did the only thing she could do, she pulled away.

CHAPTER 14

*T*yler sat on the plush, white sofa in the middle of the Talvato's living room holding his guitar in his lap. It was near midnight and the remains of his evening lay discarded on the lamp table and the floor next to the him. Five empty bottles of Stella, an empty pizza box, and a half eaten bag of vanilla wafers laying on the couch next to him. That was the extent of his social life.

Tyler didn't care if the place was a mess or if he looked like a pathetic loner on this Saturday night. He was on a roll.

Tyler's music didn't always come to him easily. It usually needed time, sometimes alcohol, and almost always required some kind of strong emotion to push him over the edge into songwriting mode. Julia had supplied that earlier today.

He could close his eyes and still feel her fingers in his hair, her breath on his neck, the heat of her body pushing against his own. He knew she was married. He'd been talking to her husband just a few minutes before he was holding her in his arms in their kitchen. It's not that he didn't care that she was married, he just couldn't help how she made him feel.

Tyler wasn't sure he would have stopped himself if she hadn't pulled away from him. His hands touched her without asking his permission. His body was always turning towards her, always moving closer than was appropriate. Then when she'd started crying, he'd lost any ability to follow social norms.

Right now he didn't care. Holding her felt like the only right thing that had happened to him in a long time, maybe ever, and he would have done it all over again if given the chance. Now there was the memory of it, and the ache. The deep ache inside of him that lurched and burned hot every time he let himself relive those few moments, which was nearly constantly since he'd left the party.

He played the tune that had been forming in his mind all night. The notes were beautiful and sad, perfectly reflecting the way she had looked at him in the kitchen. She had pressed her hands against his chest and pushed him gently away. Her hazel eyes wet with tears and glistening as she stood there searching his face, for what he didn't know.

What he did know was that it had taken every bit of will power he possessed to release her from his arms. She had stepped away from him, and in order to keep his hands from reaching for her he'd shoved them into his pockets. They stood barely apart for what felt like the longest time until Tyler spoke, "Are you all right?"

The sound of his voice broke through the charm that kept them gazing at each other. Julia smiled, and looked bashfully at the floor, "I'm fine. Everything's fine. I guess I'm a little stressed." She looked back at him, her eyes shining, "Thank you."

Now Tyler was put on the spot and he felt heat rising in his cheeks at the gratefulness in her voice. He shuffled his feet like a schoolboy and mumbled something incoherent.

Then, jamming his hands further into his pockets, he shrugged, "I can't handle crying. It does something to me."

The truth was he could handle crying with anyone else, but he'd never felt such a strong reaction to tears as he did with Julia. He wanted to protect her, hold her, and make her sadness disappear.

As the memories of the day continued to wash over him, Tyler strummed his guitar and took the time to scribble some notes on a pad of paper. Frito, still wearing his red bandanna, ran in the room and hopped up on the couch next to him.

"Well, Frito," Tyler said to the little dog who perked his ears and cocked his head to listen, "It looks like I might be in trouble with this one." Frito barked twice then whined. "Yeah, I know." Tyler leaned back against the couch and took a swig out of his last beer. Frito barked again, "Oh, sorry buddy." Tyler reached into the bag of cookies and pulled out a vanilla wafer, breaking a piece off of the edge, "Here you go." Tyler tossed the treat to Frito who caught it expertly in his tiny jaws. The little dog laid down and munched happily as Tyler played his song from the very beginning and sang the lyrics that were scrawled on the notepad.

> "Where are you now love, where have you been,
> Are you waiting for me in the eyes of a friend..."

CHAPTER 15

*J*ulia could hear Jim raising his voice at the children downstairs. His plane was late arriving at the airport, and he's been rushed ever since he got home. He was still in office mode, which made him more stern than normal, plus they were probably going to be late for their dinner reservation.

Today was their anniversary. They were married fourteen years ago this afternoon. Jim called her earlier in the week from Chicago to tell her that he made reservations at Scalini Fedeli, a beautiful Italian restaurant in Chatham, and a bit of a tradition for them over the past few years.

She was in the bathroom, finishing her hair before she put on her heels. It was always a little stressful trying to get out of the house for an evening alone. It was like the kids could sense that they were about to be abandoned and they ended up fighting with each other just as she and Jim were walking out the door. Tonight was a little different because they weren't fighting. They were loud and disorderly because they were excited that Tyler was coming over to babysit.

It had been Jim's idea. When he called with the anniversary plans, Julia was a little taken aback. Over the past few years she'd grown used to a lack of attention from her husband overall, so she hadn't given much thought to their anniversary. When he'd told her to get a sitter she could not come up with anyone who might be available right off the top of her head.

"Why not that Tyler kid?" Jim asked. "The kids like him, and he's right next door. Do you trust him Jules?" Of course she trusted him, and she said she would ask him the next time she saw him. So it was all settled.

Now Julia stood in front of the full length mirror in her bedroom smoothing her hand over the classically cut black dress she'd bought at Christmas when she and her sister, Maggie, had gone on a shopping spree. Maggie encouraged her to buy this more fitted dress, insisting that the extra curves she had gained since having Sarah were well earned and quite attractive.

Now Julia wasn't so sure.

She was slightly ashamed that the prospect of wearing the tight fitting dress in front of Jim wasn't the problem. She dreaded making an appearance in something that might make her look fat not because she was worried about her own husband, but because she wanted to impress Tyler.

She opted to wear no stockings since it was summer, but was trying out Spanx for the first time ever with this dress. Spanx were super tight, girdle like, full body underwear that promised all around smoothing without "smush". She stood sideways in the mirror to see if they were working. Not too bad.

Still, she was sure Tyler was used to "hot" young women, the kind that didn't have to suck in their stomachs or wear Spanx—at least not yet. They were smooth and firm and round in just the right places. Their skin had no wrinkles, their hair was long and lush, and the natural look still worked for them. They wore bikinis, plunging necklines, strapless dresses, mini skirts and glittery stiletto heels to accentuate their perfectly muscular rumps.

She sighed. This was silly. What did it matter if Tyler liked her dress anyway? She was going out with her *husband* for their *anniversary* for heaven's sake. Tyler Hughes was just a charming, extremely attractive, sexy–very sexy–young man who was spending the summer in the house next door. He only talked with her because he was bored. She was a distraction from him spending the day watching reality TV or sleeping, nothing more.

Julia was slipping on her shoes when she heard the door-bell ring and the resulting commotion from the kids. Her stomach flipped and her hands felt clammy. She looked worriedly at her reflection again, and decided to take a minute to compose herself while Jim handled everything downstairs.

Sitting on the bed she took a few deep breaths. "Focus," she said to herself out loud, "on your anniversary." Julia stood up in front of the mirror again and looked into her own eyes, "You've been married for fourteen years today, to a wonderful man."

"Jules," Jim was yelling up the stairs, "Are you ready? We're going to be late!"

"A wonderful marriage to a wonderful man." Julia turned away from the mirror, picked up her handbag from the dresser and walked out the bedroom door.

CHAPTER 16

*T*yler didn't fumble too noticeably, he hoped, while exchanging pleasantries with Julia's husband. When he showed up as the babysitter Randy and Nicky were ready to tackle him as he came in the door so conversation was limited, which was fine with Tyler.

He was also secretly pleased to take note that he had a few inches on Jim, standing a little taller and, in his humble opinion, sporting a better hair cut than the older man too. As Jim asked him polite questions and Tyler answered while picking up the boys one by one and tossing them lightly on the couch, Tyler found himself wondering how much Jim made every year.

All thoughts, jealous or not, about Jim disappeared when Julia appeared at the top of the wide staircase that curved slightly into the living room. She was dressed in a killer black dress that hugged every part of her shapely figure and was cut above her knees, revealing her long legs that Tyler realized he had never seen in high heels before. As he watched her descend the staircase everything seemed to go into slow motion. He lost track of the kids running around the living room and his conversation with Jim.

Luckily, Jim was distracted scolding the boys for being rowdy, but Tyler could barely hear it for the sound of his own heartbeat. Julia watched him watch her, and he felt like the swing of her hips, the tracing of her fingers down the wooden railing, and the sexy way she pushed a lock of hair behind her ear, were meant just for him.

"You look beautiful," Jim spoke the words that Tyler had been thinking, which brought him out of his head and back into the room where he realized he was gawking at another man's wife. Tyler ran his hand nervously through his hair then jammed his hands into his pockets, not sure he could keep himself from touching Julia.

"Thank you," Julia smiled as she reached the bottom of the stairs and took the hand that Jim offered her. She glanced back at Tyler, "How are you, Tyler?"

Tyler began to stammer an answer when he felt a tapping on his leg and heard Sarah saying his name in baby language, "Dy-dy-dy". They all looked down to see Sarah reaching up towards Tyler, straining to be picked up.

Thankful for the interruption, he bent down quickly and swooped her up in his arms, "Hey, I found a little girl!" Sarah squealed as he dipped her up and down as if she was on a tiny roller coaster.

All that was left to do was to watch Jim escort Julia out the door, which Tyler endured bravely, using jokes and messing with the kids to distract himself from the sick feeling in the pit of his stomach.

He stood in the open front door with Sarah, holding her arm and making it wave madly at her Mom and Dad as they strolled to their SUV. Sarah laughed so hard at this game that he couldn't help but smile and he kept his good humor as he played with the kids all evening. Not once did he give in to the pang of misery that flared up every time he thought about Julia out on the town, in that dress, with Jim.

～

Later, she woke him up.

Tyler was laying back in the rose colored reclining chair that sat next to Sarah's crib in the nursery. Sarah was nestled against his chest and he had one arm protectively around her, even in his sleep.

He didn't wake up right away because Julia was speaking so softly. Her voice entered his dream and he turned towards the sound of it then was pulled completely awake to find her leaning over him and her slumbering daughter in the dark room.

"Tyler...Tyler," Julia had her hand on his shoulder and for a moment Tyler couldn't remember where he was and thought he might still be dreaming. He wasn't.

"Hey," he made a move to sit up, but Sarah wiggled in protest.

"No, you don't have to get up." Julia was talking in an almost whisper. She moved a pink and white checked stool next to the recliner and sat down keeping one hand on Sarah's back to soothe the little girl with her touch. "How did everything go?"

"Fine, fine," Tyler felt a little foggy. He let his head rest back on the chair, "Sorry, she kept waking up. I must have dozed off."

Julia shook her head slightly, "That's okay, it's sweet." She glanced at the guitar leaning against the wall, "Were you playing for her?"

Tyler followed her gaze and nodded, "I didn't know how to get her to go to sleep."

"Yeah," Julia looked tenderly at her daughter as she patted her back, "she can be a bear."

He took in all of it, the warmth of Sarah sleeping on his chest, the enchanting expression on Julia's face so close to him in the dark, the intimacy of it all. Tyler stayed very still, wanting this moment to go on forever and feeling that if he moved, if he even breathed, it would all disappear. Julia's gaze moved from the back of Sarah's sleeping head to Tyler's hand resting next to her own on Sarah's back.

Tyler watched her face as her eyes traveled down his arm, over his shoulder, along his jawline and finally rested on his mouth. He could see her lips part ever so slightly in the dim light of the room and felt his pulse immediately speed up. She caught herself staring and looked up into his eyes. She seemed almost startled.

Tyler didn't want to scare her away. He tried to act nonchalant, "How was dinner?"

"Dinner? It was good," she looked briefly towards the well lit hallway, "Jim's gone to bed. He's exhausted."

"Are you tired?"

Julia looked back at him with a twinge of a mischievous grin, "No, I think I'm a little tipsy."

"Oh," he chuckled, "a little wine with dinner?" Julia nodded, her eyes twinkling at him. She was happy and relaxed, the way he liked to see her. He watched her fingers lightly touch the curls in Sarah's hair. They sat together that way for a few minutes.

"Have you always played music?" Julia asked him.

"Yes," he answered, "well, since I was 10."

There was a slight pause and then, "Do you love it?"

"Yeah, I do."

"That's good," Julia appeared to be talking to him and thinking about something else at the same time, "You should do what you love."

Tyler watched her for a moment then asked, "What do you love to do?" He could feel her tense slightly at the question.

"I've got the kids." It was a half statement. Tyler waited. "I like gardening." He could tell that she was deciding to say something else, so he waited. "Once," her voice was quieter, "before the kids and the house...before I was married, I used to love to draw. You know, drawing and painting." Julia looked at him for a response. Tyler nodded in support. "I don't really do it anymore. No time."

"You should," Tyler said.

Julia shrugged, a slight melancholy shadow falling over her face, "It's kind of silly, really, in the grand scheme of things."

"It's not silly, Julia. You should do what you love." She looked at him appreciatively and he hoped that she could tell that he meant it.

CHAPTER 17

*J*im had known this was coming for a while, so he found it interesting that he was nervous. He wasn't a man prone to getting butterflies, but he supposed that it was natural given the circumstances.

He stood alone in the slick elevator rushing him to the 25th floor, the floor that housed the office of Stephen Cole, the CEO of his company. The walls of the elevator were covered in alternating vertical thick strips of dark wood and mirrors. He took a moment to glance at his reflection in one of the mirror strips to make sure that his tie was straight. It was.

Once on the 25th floor Jim waited patiently for the secretary to announce his presence to the room full of company executives who were waiting for him. He didn't have to wait long. With an efficiency that only comes from highly paid administrative assistants, Jim was ushered into the elegant conference room adjacent to Stephen's office and the meeting commenced.

They had been grooming him for this promotion for a

few years now. The title of Director of Operations of the Eastern Division came with a lot more money, a bigger office, and a moving bonus. It was an achievement, and one that he accepted with pride as well a good amount of relief. It would finally make sense to move his family to Chicago and end the stress that all of this traveling put on his marriage.

Jim wasn't oblivious to the distance growing between he and Julia these past few years. The slow disintegration of what used to be their natural ability to communicate, the dark fatigue that wrapped around them after the kids were in bed and they were alone, and most recently, their inability to connect in bed, were all things Jim was concerned with but had been forced to put off handling until he had this promotion in the bag.

Now it was settled. The position was his and it felt good to shake hands with Stephen in front of the other executives. They even had the company photographer snap a picture that would appear in their internal newsletter. He would take a copy to Julia. She would be excited, he was certain, and he hoped it would get her out of the strange fogginess that had been engulfing her lately.

After their semi-strained anniversary dinner, he felt like Julia was feeling a little down. He knew that he'd been tired and unsocial that night and she felt it. She was gloomy most of the evening and ended up drinking more wine than normal. It was all rushed and didn't feel that celebratory, and Jim felt like the accomplishment of a fourteen year marriage was worthy of more festivity.

He would make up for it this time, when he broke the big news to her. He'd do flowers and dinner and whatever else might put a smile on her face. He missed that smile, and now he was in a position to fix it.

Jim grinned from ear to ear as the other company Directors gathered around him, slapping him on the back and promising drinks on them that night and a round of golf the next time they had a chance. It must all have been more important to him than he realized, because Jim could still feel a knot of nerves sitting in his stomach. That was odd, he thought his tension would have dissipated by now.

CHAPTER 18

*W*hen Julia opened the front door she was greeted with an enormous bouquet of balloons. They were so plentiful that she couldn't make out who was holding them until she heard Tyler's voice calling out to her, "Happy Birthday!"

Julia was delighted and speechless. How did Tyler know it was her birthday?

They were interrupted by Randy, "Whoa! Mom, those are for you?"

"Yes!" Tyler poked his head awkwardly around the edge of the balloons, "It's your birthday, isn't it?"

Julia stepped back allowing Tyler to enter, "Yes, but how did you know?"

"I didn't," Tyler admitted, "The delivery guy brought these to my door by mistake."

Julia laughed and didn't have time to be too disappointed that Tyler hadn't psychically figured out her birthday before Nicky and Sarah joined them and there was an outburst of glee over the balloons. Nicky celebrated by standing on one end of the couch and doing forward flips to the opposite side, over and over again.

"Nice, Nickodemus!" Tyler took a moment to be impressed with the little boy's athletic ability then he handed the bunch of balloons that were handily tied to a basket full of cookies and brownies to Julia.

"Thank you." Julia beamed.

Tyler reached into his back pocket and pulled out a card, handing it to Julia with a flourish, "This came with it."

Inside the card Julia found a lovely note from Maggie along with a coupon for a spa day at a local place that Maggie frequented when she came to visit them. The kids decided that she should have a cookie from her basket and they all ended up in the kitchen munching treats and admiring the balloons.

After learning who had sent her the basket Tyler was full of questions about Maggie and Julia told him stories of her wild, photographer sister who was always full of crazy ideas and good humor. Randy took Julia's card out to put on the refrigerator and noticed the spa coupon, "What's this, Mom?"

"Oh, it's a spa day from Aunt Maggie."

"What's a spa day?"

"It's where you go and have your nails done and get a massage and all kinds of fancy stuff."

"Girlie stuff?" Nicky asked as he rummaged through the basket looking for more goodies.

"Yes," Julia smiled, "girlie stuff."

"Nice," Tyler said, "When are you going to go?"

"Oh, I don't know." She looked around at the kids and the dishes that still hadn't been done from breakfast and, despite all of the recent excitement, Julia felt a wave of sadness come over her, "I don't know if I'll have the time." Stupid, she thought, I'm just feeling sorry for myself.

Randy wrapped his arm around her shoulder, "You

should go, Mom. It's your birthday." Julia realized that she was staring at her lap and she looked up to give Randy a reassuring smile. When she turned her gaze to Tyler she saw that he was watching Randy.

Suddenly, Tyler smacked his hand on the table. Everyone looked at him, "Now that I know it's your birthday I'm ashamed to say I didn't get you anything." Tyler stood up in a mock display of seriousness, "Therefore I am making a decision." Julia and the kids all waited, "I am giving you a free day of babysitting on your birthday!" There was a moment's pause before Nicky started shouting something about getting the light sabers from his bedroom and ran out of the kitchen.

"Oh, you don't--" Julia started to speak, but Tyler would hear nothing of it.

"No, *this*," he made a wide sweeping motion with his arm, "is happening. You go to the spa, I'll watch the kids."

"Yeah, Mom," Randy piped in. Sarah clapped her hands and bent her knees up and down in a kind of baby dance to show her enthusiasm. "See?" Randy said, "Even Sarah wants you to go."

Twenty minutes later Julia was pulling out of the driveway, waving at Tyler and the kids who watched her from the doorway. She had her spa coupon in her purse and an appointment for a facial, massage and mani-pedi that Tyler had set up on the phone while she was changing clothes. She was on a bit of a high after spending such a whirlwind morning with him, and she only felt the tiniest bit of guilt for leaving him in charge of a messy house and three rowdy kids.

Tyler, for his part, was quite pleased with himself. Upon seeing Julia's expression once she realized she was going to have a day of relaxation he immediately started devising another plan.

As soon as her SUV was out of sight Nicky turned to him and said, "I got the light sabers! Time to fight!"

"No, Nicky, I've got another idea."

The masseuse, a thickly built blonde man named Gil, worked on her shoulders and back, gently kneading her taunt muscles. Julia felt some of the tension that seemed to be with her constantly these days slip away.

She already felt more pampered and calm than she had in years after spending a few hours in this relaxing environment. She puttered around to the different rooms of the spa in her puffy, white bathrobe and slippers that they provided, received her facial, luxury mani-pedi and now a soothing Swedish massage.

The spa ladies fed her herbal tea, fresh oatmeal cookies, bottled water and a protein bar at different junctures of her time there and chatted with her about her kids, her husband and, after some coaxing, Tyler. This environment, much like a hair salon, lent itself to talking about womanly secrets. She felt compelled to tell the story of the gorgeous young man who had made this whole day possible for her.

Now, with the quiet music floating around her and the sensual feeling of Gil's strong, warm hands moving over her whole body, Julia closed her eyes and let herself think about Tyler. Her mind drifted to the moment she'd seen him peek around the balloons and she felt a flutter in her stomach. Then, to keep the feeling going, she thought back to when he had embraced her in the kitchen. Now the rest of her body started responding to the thought of Tyler and, she noticed, to Gil's insistent fingers.

Even though her eyes were closed, she could tell that he was standing directly in front of her head and shoulders, leaning into the table and sliding his hands up and down the middle of her back. Keeping one hand on her at all times, he moved to her side, slipping his hand down her body, past her waist, then moving the light sheet that covered her rump to expose even more of her lower back.

For an instant Julia allowed herself to think about Gil moving the sheet all of the way off of her and slipping his hand and persistent fingers between her legs. She felt her body respond to just the thought of this and wondered briefly what she would do if he actually did it. She smiled for a second because she knew the answer–she would flip out.

She must have chuckled at the thought because Gil asked her, "Does that tickle?"

"No," she answered, "it's fine."

Gil continued with the Swedish massage as Julia composed herself and decided not to think about any man while she was in this state of undress.

The house was silent when Julia arrived back home. She figured that everyone was out back or maybe even over at Tyler's playing with Frito. She was so relaxed. Every inch of her body was soft and the multitude of different lotions, oils and treatments that she had sampled at the spa left her happy and smelling, she thought, quite fantastic.

As she walked through the living room towards the kitchen she noticed that all of the toys were picked up. Everything seemed really spiffy, actually, neater than when she had left. She smiled and thought to herself, Tyler is amazing.

Just at that moment, she walked into the kitchen and Tyler with Sarah in his arms, Randy holding a wiggling Frito, and Nicky all jumped out at her and yelled, "Happy Birthday!" Julia halted in surprise at the shouting and yipping from Frito, who was wearing a bow originally meant for a present on his head. It took her a moment to see past the jubilance. When she finally did, she noticed that there was an elaborate birthday celebration waiting for her on the kitchen table.

Her giant balloon bouquet from earlier was still tied to its basket and sitting in the middle of the table. There was also a multi layered white birthday cake with blobs of green and pink icing decorating the top sitting next to it. The cake was crooked, leaning precariously to one side and reminded her of a Dr. Seuss drawing. Next to the cake sat a gift wrapped in bright purple paper with a giant pink polka dotted bow stuck on top. The bow was more than half the size of the gift.

"We made you a cake!" Nicky was beside himself.

Randy stood proudly by the table, "Happy Birthday, Mom!"

"Thank you!" Julia looked at all of them, Randy, Nicky, Tyler and Sarah. Sarah squealed in delight then reached out to her mother. Julia moved towards Tyler to take her daughter, but couldn't take her eyes off of him.

His eyes were shining as he stepped towards her to hand over Sarah, "Happy Birthday," he said softly as he shifted Sarah into Julia's open arms. He put his free hand on Julia's waist and leaned over to give her a quick peck on the cheek. It was so fast the boys didn't see him do it, but Julia blushed happily as Tyler pulled away, "Man, you smell good." He stated. Julia blushed even harder.

The birthday party officially commenced. Julia followed all of the instructions from the boys about where to sit and what to do. All of them took perfect care of her as she watched with great delight. Sarah had the job of passing out the little cone birthday hats to everyone. Tyler helped Randy light candles on the cake, and they all sang to her as she blew them out. Randy explained how they had baked the cake themselves, with Tyler's help, and that's why it was a little crooked. Julia told him it was a beautiful birthday cake and took a picture of it with her phone.

Nicky presented her with an oversized, homemade birthday card that they all made together. There was a drawing of stick figures wearing birthday hats surrounding a huge white and green and pink birthday cake that was just slightly more crooked than the real one. There was even a little scribble with a bow on top representing Frito, she guessed. They had all, even Sarah, signed their names inside of the card. Julia took a few minutes to admire it before Nicky announced it was time for her present.

"I get a present, too?" Julia exclaimed as they laid it in front of her.

"Well, Tyler had to buy it," Randy confessed.

Julia was surprised and she looked at Tyler, "You didn't have to buy a present."

"Oh, it's from all of us," Tyler answered, "Everyone helped pick it out."

Julia felt the heat rising in her cheeks as she carefully removed the gigantic bow and tore open the purple wrapping. "I hope you like it." Tyler said as he watched.

Inside the wrapping paper was a sleek wooden box that, when she opened it, revealed compartments holding a variety of different high quality drawing supplies. Colored pencils, charcoal pencils, graphite pencils, soft and hard pastels, and anything she could have ever imagined needing or wanting to draw. She forgot, for a moment, that everyone was watching her as she ran her fingers over the utensils.

"Look what else!" Nicky reached under the wooden box where there were two artist sketchbooks of different qualities of paper, "We got you stuff to draw pictures!" She could tell that Nicky thought this was the best gift they could have ever gotten her and, in a way, it was.

"Do you like them?" Randy asked, "Tyler said he thought you might like to draw with grown up stuff."

Julia smiled at her oldest son, "Yes, Randy, these are just beautiful." She looked at Tyler. She tried to say 'Thank you' but the words held in her throat. She was afraid she might cry again.

Perhaps sensing her emotional reaction, or realizing that the kids weren't going to leave the drawing supplies alone for long, Tyler spoke up, "Come on, let's get some plates and have some cake!"

Julia watched him take command of the little kids and turn the whole cake cutting and serving into a great big game. She felt as if she was sitting back watching a scene from a movie or through a glass window. It was her family, but it wasn't. Julia placed her hand on the clean, unused pencils lined up neatly in their box and it seemed to her as if the whole room turned a little brighter.

CHAPTER 19

*I*t was after 11:00pm. Jim's key turned in the lock and he pushed open the front door expecting to find a dark house. Instead he saw Julia curled up on the couch under a blanket, bathed in flickering blue light from the television. There was a movie playing on TV. The volume was low. Julia was asleep.

He placed his suitcase next to the wall and quietly shut and locked the door. His tie was already loosened around his neck and he'd unbuttoned his cuffs and rolled up the sleeves of his shirt hours ago during the heat of the afternoon. The house was nicely cool thanks to the air conditioning.

Jim was tired, really tired. It had been a long day at work and an even longer commute home on the plane, delays in the airline and other such nonsense. It was good to be home.

He kicked off his shoes and walked softly to the couch. Julia looked so cozy he hated to wake her, but it had been over a week since he'd been home. She must have been waiting up for him, even though he told her not to when he called from the airport and left a message.

Jim lifted the blanket from off of her feet and sat down on

the couch, lifting her bare feet onto his lap and covering both her feet and his lap back up with the blanket. He ran his hand over her toes, her heel and up her calf. Her skin was warm and smooth and he could feel some of the tension release from his back and shoulders just by touching her.

She stirred and moved her feet in his hands. He responded by rubbing them more firmly. Julia moaned almost imperceptibly and Jim was suddenly aroused. Her feet pushed harder into his lap and he responded just like a husband who hadn't seen his wife in a while would be expected to respond.

With one hand on her feet he let his free hand wander up her leg farther and farther, taking his time and relishing every inch of her supple skin. She continued to react to his hands so sensually that anyone else might think she was awake, but Jim knew that she wasn't. After fourteen years together he could tell when his wife was asleep. He did, however, wonder what she was dreaming about.

Whatever was going on in her mind was obviously hot and it was making him hot. As he let his hands roam freely over her body she pressed against them, made soft noises of pleasure, and at one point he even heard her speak someone's name. It wasn't his.

He moved her over on the couch to make enough room to lay next to her under the blanket. Her eyes fluttered open and she focused on him, finally awake, "Hi Babe," he said. Before she had a chance to answer him, he kissed her, relishing in her warm, full lips and waiting for that magical moment when they opened for him and let him push his tongue into her sweet mouth.

Under the blanket his hands were confident of where to go and what to do in order to give her pleasure. Within a few moments Julia's eyes were closed again but not because she was sleeping. He kissed her neck, pulled her shirt up and ran his hands over her naked breasts. She tilted her head back, giving him full access to her neck. At the same moment her legs opened allowing him to push easily in between them. Now it was his turn to moan.

"The kids," she whispered.

"They're asleep," Jim answered into her neck. His fingers found the waistband of the boxer shorts she was so fond of sleeping in and he slipped his hand inside, finally reaching the hot, slick prize that waited there. "Oh, God, Jules."

That was all it took. The rest was a blur to him, a pounding, rushing, hot blur until Jim found her completely nude under him, his pants pulled down enough to expose his hardness, but only for a moment, because before she could protest that the kids might wake up he plunged deep into her, the slippery heat enveloping him, and he lost himself in the deliciousness of his wife.

Afterwards they lay together on the couch, still completely covered by the blanket. Julia nestled in his arms, fully awake now, but quiet.

"It's been a while since we've done it out here," she sounded amused. Jim chuckled and kissed her hair. "What if the kids had walked in?" Julia smacked his chest in a mock act of discipline.

"They didn't," he answered, "and we had a blanket." He couldn't tell if she was agreeing or not since her face was hidden from him. Then he was struck with a thought, "Hey, who's Gil?"

"What?"

"Gil, who's Gil?"

"Is this like a knock-knock joke?"

"No," Jim laughed, "You said someone's name when you were asleep. You were dreaming." Julia grew very still and didn't answer him, "Were you having a sex dream about someone named Gil?"

Julia pulled away from him, "What? Why would you ask me something like that?"

"I'm not upset or anything." He offered.

"What did I say when I was asleep?"

"I don't know," Jim was surprised at her strong reaction, "You said something like 'Yes, Gil'...when I was touching you." Julia blushed deeply and buried her face back in his chest. "You were having a hot dream weren't you, Babe?" He asked, still amused.

"I'm sorry," he heard her voice, muffled against him.

Jim laughed again and squeezed her tight, "You don't have to apologize. It was a dream." Julia didn't answer him. "You can dream all night long about some schmuck named Gil, as long as I'm the one who gets to wake up with you. Besides, it was pretty sexy."

Julia stayed silent, wrapped in his arms, and he thought that he might tell her about his promotion, but it didn't seem like the time. He wanted to keep this feeling of closeness around them for as long as he could. Talking about work didn't seem to be the way to do that. Anyway, he was tired, and soon sleep would take them over.

CHAPTER 20

*J*ulia was so angry she didn't hear the waiter, not
until Jim spoke her name and even then he had
to say it twice. Finally she looked up from her
plate and saw the waiter poised to refill her wine glass. She
nodded and watched the deep, red wine pour until it had
reached the perfect spot about a third of the way from the
rim. As soon as he was finished, Julia took up the glass and
brought it to her lips, letting the heat of the wine fill her
mouth and burn her throat.

She wasn't drunk, as Jim had just accused her of being,
but she had a feeling she would be by the end of the night.

It was infuriating. The way he sat across the table and
glared at her like she was a young child, like she was one of
their children! Even though they were surrounded by an
elegant atmosphere, glittering tableware and gourmet food,
Julia still felt like a naughty little girl who was being repri-
manded by her father.

They sat in silence, Jim's jaw set rigidly, the initial gaiety
of her belated birthday dinner squelched for the rest of the
evening. That was another thing, Julia allowed the hurt and

anger from yesterday resurface, how could her own husband completely forget her birthday?

After their rendezvous on the couch they both fell asleep and awakened very early in the morning, Jim because he was hungry and Julia because she was uncomfortable. They decided to get a snack and when they walked into the kitchen the look of astonishment on Jim's face at the sight of the balloons was enough for Julia to know that he had forgotten.

She was so busy at the spa and with Tyler and the kids all day that she hadn't really taken time to think about Jim. He was due back in the evening and she decided to wait up for him. It wasn't unusual for him to be delayed on his flight home, nor was it unusual for him to not make a fuss about her birthday until he got home from work. It was unusual, however, for him to forget it entirely.

Of course, he was sorry. He was contrite, apologized profusely, called himself an uncaring jerk. He'd felt even worse after seeing all of the work the boys, with Tyler's help, had gone to make her a cake and a card, and he promised to make it all up to her the next night with a fancy dinner and an overnight stay in a great hotel.

She had agreed. Everything had seemed all right. With his work schedule and being gone so much, they were so out of synch with each other that the idea of her birthday slipping his mind wasn't completely outlandish. Besides, she'd really had a great birthday without his input so she didn't feel the right to complain much.

Inside, however, she felt numb. Stunned, like when she was a kid and Maggie would play that game of slapping the inside of her forearm until it was red. She knew that it stung more than she could actually feel at the moment. The cold, numbness was there to protect her, she supposed, to keep her from feeling the full jolt of pain. That would come later.

They left for her belated birthday celebration pleasantly. No snags, no quarrels, not until Jim decided to announce to her over their entrees that he was planning on moving their entire family to Chicago. It wasn't just the news, it was the way he said it, with such surety, such control, as if her opinion in the matter didn't count for anything. That's what sent her over the edge, snapping at him, enraged at the idea of leaving her home. Then he went and accused her of being drunk.

The wine glass was still in her hand and she saw that she had downed a great deal of her refill. Julia placed it on the white tablecloth and put her hands in her lap. She sighed, feeling sick more than angry now, and looked up at her husband.

Jim was staring at a far corner of the restaurant. He wasn't really looking at anything, just staring. The clenching in his jaw had ceased and he didn't look angry anymore. He looked tired, worn out, from what she wasn't sure. And he looked old. Julia wondered if she looked old and tired, sitting mutely at a candlelight dinner with her husband.

"Are you ready to go?" She asked. Her voice sounded more rough than she meant it to. Jim looked at her blankly, then glanced around at the table.

"Don't you want any dessert?"

"No," she tried to smile at him, "Not really. I'm a little tired."

Jim looked slightly wounded, but not totally surprised. He sighed, "Okay." He motioned to the waiter and dinner was over.

Later Julia lay in a strange bed listening to her husband sleep. Her back was to him, her pillow was folded under her cheek, and she gripped it with both hands. She stared into the darkness of the hotel room. It was so dark she couldn't see even the outline of the furniture.

In the blackness she felt safe because nobody was looking, and even if they were they couldn't truly see her. She felt the hard knot in the pit of her stomach wrench and she took a deep breath, letting it out slowly and allowing the knot to loosen. As it relaxed the sadness welled up in her throat, then her mouth, then behind her eyes, pressing against them with such force she couldn't take another breath. Without another moment to pause and think, it began pouring out of her and into the night that surrounded her.

She lay quietly next to Jim, tears streaming down her face in one continuous flow, soaking into the soft, white linen on her folded pillow.

Once they started she couldn't stop them if she tried, but there was no reason to try. Jim couldn't hear her. No one could see her. She was invisible in the darkness, alone with the mess inside of her heart.

CHAPTER 21

*S*arah's small hand gripped Tyler's forefinger tightly as the water approached their bare feet. They stood on the beach just inside the reach of the wave's edge, where salty water wrapped around their ankles with a froth of bubbles and playfully pulled the sand out from under their toes. Sarah giggled uncontrollably as the waves slid towards them and away again. The movement of the water was dizzying and Tyler could feel Sarah totter each time a wave pulled back into the ocean.

He squatted behind the little girl to put his hand on her waist and steady her a bit more. She held fast to his finger and looked back at him with such excitement and joy that he forgot the gloomy mood he'd been fighting ever since Julia's birthday party.

"Dy, Dy, Dy!" That was the way Sarah said his name, he couldn't help but smile every time she did.

"Yeah?"

Sarah pointed her free hand at the wave that was now approaching them and squealed, "Dy!"

"I see it, here it comes!" He braced Sarah for the water to

hit her legs and realized at the last moment that this particular wave was going to be much bigger than its predecessors. He grabbed Sarah's waist with both hands and stood up, lifting her high into the air as the wave crashed against his legs, splashing water high above his waist. He brought her down and held her against him, "Whoa," he said, "that was a big one."

"Wo! Wo!" Sarah repeated gleefully, but he could feel her whole body trembling and thought maybe they'd had enough ocean waves for the moment.

"You want to go back and see Mommy?" He asked. Sarah nodded and pointed at Julia who sat on the beach blanket sketching in her sketchbook.

So they walked back towards Julia and with every step Tyler felt the gloom descending on him again. It wasn't that he didn't want to see Julia, talk to her, hear her laugh, touch her skin, or watch her moving through all of the details of her life. It was that he wanted to do all of those things so badly that every second he was with her felt charged with excitement, followed by the inevitable moment she shut the door of her house and retired to be with her family and her husband, leaving him alone.

That's when the depression set in, the realization that he was never going to be anything more to her than what he was, the neighbor, the babysitter. The question was, why did he spend all of his time with her and her kids? Why did he continue to agree to babysit, even when it was Jim asking him to babysit overnight so he could take her to a hotel and do God knows what?

Tyler couldn't even think about Julia and Jim together, it made him sick to his stomach. But he couldn't refuse a chance to see her, be around her, even being in her house somehow made him feel better *and* worse. This was crazy. It was something he'd never experienced before, this feeling of being drawn to a woman uncontrollably, his mood so dependent on her presence in his life.

He and Sarah made their way back to Julia, the sound of the waves rolling rhythmically in and out kept them company as they walked, and Tyler decided that his unobstructed view of Julia sketching in the sun was worth any pain that it might cause him to part from her later in the day.

She'd developed a nice tan over the past weeks, and filled out her swimsuit so well he sometimes found it difficult not to stare at her curves. In order to draw in the bright sunshine Julia was sporting sunglasses and a floppy straw hat, which Tyler found utterly charming. It wasn't just the hat, it was the fact that she was so enjoying her birthday present, it made him feel close to her. Little things like her funny hat, the way she painted her and Sarah's toenails the same color, the private jokes they had together, all of these added up to something Tyler didn't want to think about, something he knew he was going to have to face - eventually.

Julia looked up from her sketchbook and saw them approaching the blanket. She smiled and waved at them, "Hi, pumpkin!" Tyler knew she was talking to Sarah, but a piece of him hoped she was that happy to have him return to her as well. In that moment when she was grinning happily under her giant floppy hat, surrounded by her art supplies and seeming so pleased and content, Tyler knew that he loved her.

Her smile pierced straight into his heart and he knew that he wanted nothing more than to be near her in whatever way he could. He allowed the knowledge of their doomed future to recede so that he could experience the rush of pleasure he felt as he sat down next to her on the blanket. Sarah clambered to her mother and Julia spent a few minutes kissing Sarah's cheeks. Tyler watched as Sarah squirmed and laughed under her loving attention.

Further down the beach he could see Randy and Nicky racing each other back towards the blanket. Frito was a tiny blur running circles around them as they progressed. They had been hunting for sharks teeth and must have found something either really cool or really disgusting to be in such a hurry to return. Tyler smiled to himself and glanced down at Julia's sketchbook. He was struck by what he saw.

It was a drawing of he and Sarah holding hands on the shore of the ocean. They were facing the water, but in profile, frozen in time looking at each other and smiling. The amazing thing was that even in profile, without the luxury of drawing their whole face, Julia had captured a moment of fun and excitement between him and the little girl that was surprising to see in such a rough sketch.

She was good, really good. Tyler picked up the drawing and studied it more closely. He was not formally trained in art besides the requirements in college and the endless art and museum openings he attended with his parents as a child. But he'd come to a decision about art a long time ago, if he liked it right away he considered it good. In most cases his instincts were backed up by critical acclaim if he took the time to find out anyone else's opinions.

"I'm a little rusty." Julia stated. She had seen him looking at her work and reached to take it away from him.

"Hang on, hang on," Tyler stopped her playfully, "I think you should let me be the judge of that." She sat next to him self-consciously as he pretended to do a thorough study of her art.

"It's just a sketch." She explained.

"I think it's really good," Tyler told her again. She shook her head and blushed. "No, really! It's great, Julia!" He nudged her with his elbow and pointed to himself in the sketch, "I didn't notice Channing Tatum on the beach with us, though." Julia rolled her eyes. Tyler flipped to the previous page in the sketchbook and found an image of him, Randy and Nicky playing in the surf. Again, it was fantastic. "Wow, I'm impressed."

Julia squirmed with pleasure. "I haven't drawn in so long. It's not too bad I guess."

"No," Tyler pointed at the image of him on this page. In it he was laughing and throwing Nicky into the water. She had captured the movement very realistically and he tapped it with his finger, "I mean, I'm impressed with my six pack."

"Stop it," Julia giggled and took the sketchbook out of his hands, flipping the cover shut.

"You made me look like Aquaman or something."

Julia giggled again at the idea, "Do you even know who Aquaman is? He was a little before your time wasn't he?"

"Hey," Tyler gave her a rakish grin, "I know about a lot of things."

"Really?"

"Yep. A *lot*." At that moment the boys reached them, panting and excited to tell them about the remnants of a bonfire that they'd found under a bluff. They begged Julia to promise them a time when they could come back and have a bonfire of their own, and they included Tyler with his guitar into the mix by the time the conversation was done. Tyler was happy with the idea of spending the evening playing and singing with Julia and the kids. In fact, Tyler was happy for the first time in a very long time.

He forgot, for a while at least, that he wasn't a real member of this family, that he didn't truly live in the house next door to them, that she would be going home to lay in the arms of another man, and that there was no chance in hell that he would ever have what he wanted most in the world. In that moment he decided to ignore the fact that even though he had found love–true love–perhaps for the first time in his life, it was both forbidden and ill fated.

CHAPTER 22

*J*im didn't know how to say goodbye. He and Julia had never been in this kind of argument before, not in the history of their whole marriage. Sure, they were on speaking terms again–finally. After the fiasco of her birthday getaway they got through the cold silent stage and moved into the area of stiff, formal exchanges, enough to be civil, but that was all.

He didn't know what to do and, quite frankly, he didn't want to do anything right now. He considered taking a few days off before heading back to Chicago, but that path was fraught with trouble from his perspective. He didn't feel comfortable stepping out of the middle of the merger going on in Chicago, especially after being promoted so recently. He also could feel his own tension rising around the kids. They were getting to him. Maybe he'd gotten too used to being in the quiet of a hotel room or the structure of his office or, maybe, his wife was the one who held the whole family thing together for him.

He knew he was still angry. He hadn't expected Julia's passionate opposition to relocating to Chicago. It came as a complete surprise to him, and it made him mad—it still made him mad. Julia was a reasonable woman and she had to have known that his commuting back and forth on an airplane to work was a temporary condition. Didn't she? What did she expect? That he find another job? It was completely unrealistic and childish of her. Of course, he probably shouldn't have told her as much at her birthday dinner, but it just blurted out.

He really didn't know what to do about the whole situation. What he did know was that his plane was taking off in exactly three hours and it was high time he left for the airport. That brought him back to his current dilemma, he didn't know how to say goodbye, not with this kind of tension in the air.

Jim made his way downstairs from the bedroom where he'd been packing and placed his suitcase next to the front door. He could hear Julia in the kitchen with Sarah. The boys were outside playing in the swimming pool.

He peeked into the kitchen and saw Sarah helping Julia fill a snack tray to take outside. Julia was slicing apples and Sarah was picking up the pieces one by one, and laying them carefully in a bright plastic bowl that looked like a watermelon that had been cut in half. Sarah saw him and held up a piece of apple towards him, "DaDa!" Julia looked up.

"Thank you," Jim answered his daughter as he went to the table and took the apple piece from her little hand, gobbling is up and making funny noises for her benefit. Sarah giggled. "Mmmmm," Jim said, "Good apple." He stole a glance at Julia who was watching Sarah, "Does Mommy want an apple?"

Sarah obliged and offered Julia a slice. She took it and said, "Thank you, honey."

"So," Jim started to speak, Julia finally looked at him, her expression was flat, "I—uh—I'm leaving—my flight's leaving."

Julia nodded slightly, "Right."

There was a pause, but not a long one, because they were interrupted by Nicky who came bursting into the kitchen, soaking wet, straight from the pool, "Mom! Are the snacks ready? We're hungry!" Nicky looked at Jim, "Dad, are you coming swimming?"

"No, buddy, I can't," Jim answered, "I've gotta get to the airport."

"Oh, wait!" Nicky said, then turned around and ran to the door leading to the patio, "Randy!" He shouted as loud as he could, "Dad's leaving again!"

Jim knew that Nicky was trying to get Randy's attention to say goodbye, but his choice of words couldn't have been worse. He could feel more than see Julia's tension, and in the short amount of time left before he had to walk out the door, he decided to ignore it.

Soon Randy and Nicky were clambering into the kitchen, slipping on the tile floor with their wet feet, and ignoring all of Julia's warnings about being careful. They hugged him, Sarah hugged him and started balling when he kissed her chubby little cheek goodbye. Jim reached for Julia to give her a hug and felt her stiffen under his touch. He satisfied the moment with a quick peck on her cheek.

As he walked out of the kitchen towards the front door, Jim turned back around and said, "I'll be back Friday night."

Julia didn't say anything as she looked down at the apples in front of her and started slicing them again. Jim was pushed out the door both by time and by a feeling that he wasn't really invited to stay. With suitcase in hand he walked out of his home with more relief than he would feel comfortable admitting to anyone.

CHAPTER 23

The bonfire was set for Wednesday evening. Julia's mood slowly recovered after Jim left for the week. There was nothing to be done until he got home, so she settled into taking care of the preparations and spending more and more time with Tyler under the guise of "planning".

In reality, there wasn't that much planning that needed to be done for a bonfire, but the kids were having fun with Tyler around, and she just couldn't come up with any good reason why he shouldn't be at her house day and night. That's what it was, day and night, and Julia was thoroughly enjoying him. She knew that she was throwing herself into the experience with no thought to any consequences, but she didn't want to think about consequences right now.

Tyler was fun, and having him lounging around her swimming pool in his swim trunks was enough to keep her mind off of her troubles with Jim. There was a certain sensuality that had developed between them since her birthday. It was impossible to ignore, and she no longer wondered if he felt it too. She could feel it in the way he smoothed sunscreen over her back and in the way he stood so close to her in the kitchen, helping her make sandwiches for lunch. She could tell he liked to touch her and she liked it too. How could she not?

Tuesday night they all watched a movie together on the couch. Tyler's lean, tan body that smelled like sunshine pressed right along hers the whole time. It prevented her from keeping track of the characters on the screen. She found herself melting more and more into his body as the kids dropped off around them.

When he was sure that all the kids were asleep, Tyler put his arm around her, letting her rest her head on his chest. Julia found herself snuggling into him and only feeling the slightest bit bad about it. She drifted off listening to him breath. She felt comfortable, aroused, and better then she had in a long, long time.

Late Wednesday afternoon they made their way to the beach and claimed a good bonfire spot. They gathered wood and watched as the light dimmed on the water, the slant of the sun glinting off of the wrinkles in the waves. With a blazing bonfire, hot dogs, smores and beer for the grown ups, Julia thought this was one of the most successful outings she'd ever had with the kids–and Jim wasn't part of it. A twinge of regret flipped through her stomach and then was gone.

She wasn't going to think about Jim right now, she decided, as she opened a beer and took a swig, she was putting it out of her mind. Summer would be gone before she knew it, her kids were growing up so quickly right in front of her, and Tyler–she watched him helping Nicky assemble a smore as Sarah looked on with great interest–Tyler would be gone soon, too. Julia didn't want to mar whatever was happening between them with her feelings about Jim, or lack thereof. It wasn't exactly innocent–but technically she wasn't having an affair and she loved how he made her feel.

Julia took another drink, "Are you going to play?" She asked Tyler.

He leapt up from where he sat with Nicky, "Absolutely!"

She loved his enthusiasm. He was always up to the challenge, no matter what it was. It was invigorating to be around.

"Play my song!!" Nicky called out. He's another one for enthusiasm, Julia smiled to herself.

"Easy now, Nickelback." Tyler said as he carried his guitar case closer to Julia so he could sit down next to her, "How about we let your Mom pick the first song?"

All three of her children looked to her, their faces sticky with marshmallows, "I'd like to hear something that Tyler wrote." Julia replied. Tyler nodded as he positioned himself as close as he could to Julia while still holding the guitar.

"Okay," Tyler cleared his throat. He seemed nervous, which Julia found charming. She picked up Sarah to sit in her lap and listen. Tyler strummed the guitar a few times, then made an adjustment to the strings, "Here goes."

The melody began, a beautiful sound that lifted from where he sat next to her and lingered in the light of the fire before floating into the darkness. It was lovely and sad–almost hypnotic. Then he began to sing, his voice, deep and husky, fit perfectly to the guitar and their surroundings. Julia was captivated as she listened to the lyrics.

> "Where are you now love, where have you
> been?
> Are you waiting for me in the eyes of a
> friend..."

She watched the firelight glowing on his face, reflecting

in his eyes as he sang. He looked like he'd forgotten they were there with him. He was so focused on the song.

"What have you done, love, why did you leave?
Did you mean "no" love, how can that be..."

Julia felt connected to him, she felt like he was singing about her, to her in fact. It sent a thrill through her heart, a warmth that made everything that didn't exist within that circle of firelight, within hearing distance of his song, disappear.

Night fell completely. Too full of excitement to be tired, Randy and Nicky reveled in playing with long sticks, poking them alternately into the coals and then into the sand. Sarah lay sleeping on a nest of blankets that Julia had arranged inside a barricade made up of coolers and logs.

The bonfire was beginning to die down and they were out of wood. "Maybe we should start packing up," Julia suggested.

Tyler jumped up, "One more round of smores!" The boys cheered. Tyler held his hand out to Julia, "Come with me to get more firewood. You boys stay right here. We'll be right back."

Julia couldn't resist. She took Tyler's hand and he gently guided her into the darkness. Her heart was pounding, she knew what he was going to do and she wasn't going to stop him. When they had gotten far enough down the beach where they could still easily see the kids near the low burning fire, but were safely veiled in the night, Tyler stopped, turned towards Julia and pulled her into his arms.

It all happened in a moment. He kissed her, his lips were warm and sweet and she lost herself in them. His arms wrapped urgently around her waist and her back, holding her tightly against his body. Julia's hands moved over the muscles of his shoulders, up the back of his neck and into his thick, dark hair. She opened her mouth to him. He tasted good.

She couldn't stop kissing him. She had to stop kissing him.

Julia put her hand gently on Tyler's cheek and ran her fingers along his jaw. His lips were firm and insistent, but she pulled back from them. Tyler followed her and then stopped when she laid her fingers on his mouth.

"Wait," Julia whispered.

"Julia," his voice came from deep within him, it was quiet, throaty.

"Wait," Julia moved her other hand to his chest and gradually moved his body away from hers, "I think we should go back." She glanced back towards the bonfire, then at Tyler, "We need to go back."

Tyler was silent. He didn't argue nor pull her back into his arms. He let her move away from him, his hands sliding off of her as she walked backwards.

"I'm sorry," she said, she didn't know what else to say. Then she turned and made her way back to her children.

CHAPTER 24

Tyler twisted on the bar tool and it squeaked underneath him. He was waving good-bye to the drunk old man he'd been talking with all afternoon and into the night night. Samuel was his name and he was, as they say, three sheets to the wind. Tyler wasn't sure exactly where that saying originated, but he was certain that it applied to Samuel–and probably to him as well, if he was being perfectly honest.

But honest wasn't what he felt like at all. He didn't feel good or honest or trustworthy. He felt more like a letch than he'd ever felt before in his whole life. Letch, he chuckled out loud, that's another word he didn't really know the meaning of, but he was pretty sure he was one–a letch. Not Samuel, though. Samuel was a good man, even if he was having trouble figuring out how to open the door to get himself home.

"Tyler," Samuel told him earlier in the day, "Everyone's fallen in love with another man's wife."

"Really?" Tyler was surprised at this piece of information.

"Yep," Samuel motioned to the bartender to fill up their

shots and beers, one more round, "But a *real* man never acts on it...at least not for long." Samuel thought this was a really, really funny thing to say and spent a good five minutes in a fit of laughter over the whole thing. Tyler and Frito, who'd been allowed to sit on the barstool next to Tyler because he was that kind of dog—the carry on kind—watched Samuel snicker and snort until the next round appeared on the shiny, wooden bar in front of them. Booze seemed to calm Samuel down.

It calmed Tyler down, too. At least it dulled his senses enough that he could get over his hurt and embarrassment and spill his guts to a total stranger about his feelings for Julia and the kiss. That's what it had become now in his mind, "The Kiss".

Tyler had found his way to this neighborhood dive the night of "The Kiss", after he and Julia and the kids all returned from the beach. He tried to help Julia unload the coolers from her SUV, but she told him it was probably best if he went home. He couldn't. He found it impossible to just go back to the Talvato's big, dark house.

Instead he took Frito for a drive. With the windows down the night air cooled the car and made it so noisy that Tyler had to blast the music in order to hear anything. He didn't mind. Maybe the music and the loud wind swirling around him would make him forget. It didn't.

Eventually he found "Rudy's Lounge". It looked like the kind of place you could walk into, forget everything, and be forgotten yourself. And the bartender, Norene, took a shine to Frito.

Norene was an older woman with badly bleached hair and a penchant for tight, low cut, glittery shirts that showed off her substantial cleavage as well as her belly that drooped over the waistband of her extremely tight jeans. Tyler mused that, in her prime, Norene had been an impressive looking woman. She was still a presence to be dealt with as she clucked over Frito, feeding him bits of pretzel, even designating him his own shot glass to drink from. She called Tyler "Hun" as she half listened to his story and half watched the television that hung at one side of the bar.

Between Norene and Samuel, he and Frito found a small band of new friends who welcomed them with open arms. No judgment. No expectations. Just a seat in an air-conditioned room, a refill whenever he needed one, and a few words of wisdom from people who had, Tyler realized, experienced plenty of sadness in their own lives.

He returned to Rudy's Lounge the next day...and the next. He couldn't face being so close to Julia without being able to talk to her. He didn't know what he would do if Nicky knocked on his door wanting to play ball, or if Randy asked him if he could give him another guitar lesson, or if he saw Julia outside of her house, or if he ran into Jim pulling into the driveway.

Tyler turned back to the bar and took a deep swig of his beer. The instant he thought about any of it he felt as if he was standing on the beach with her again, her hands in his hair, her lips on his. He felt hot and restless, like he wanted to run or shout. He didn't know what to do, so he took another drink and stared at the bar.

"Last call, Hun," Norene told him, "You want anything?"

Tyler shook his head, "No, thanks." He would have to go back tonight. But he only had three weeks left at the Talvato's. He would come back to Rudy's and numb himself every day if he had to, then he would go to Austin and leave this whole situation behind him forever.

CHAPTER 25

*H*er kitchen was cleaner than it had been in years. Julia stood back and admired the gleaming stove, shining floors and glittery cabinet knobs. Her hands, protected by yellow rubber gloves, rested on her hips. Her hair was pulled into a hasty ponytail earlier in the day, which was no longer holding. Some of her bangs hung in her eyes. Julia pushed them into place with the back of her hand, careful not to touch her skin with the chemicals on the glove.

"Well," she said to the empty house, "that's better." She looked at the green, glowing numbers of the stove clock and saw the time. Was it really midnight? She looked at the clock that hung on the kitchen wall for confirmation. Yes, it was the middle of the night and she was cleaning her kitchen. She looked at the bucket of soapy water, mop and assorted bottles of cleaning solutions that sat in a neat pile next to the kitchen entrance.

"Correction," she said again to herself, "I *was* cleaning my kitchen. Now I'm going to bed." She started to peel the gloves off her hands when she noticed the top of the refrigerator, the one place she hadn't scrubbed down. A tumble of different items were shoved on top of the fridge and she knew most of them could probably be thrown away. She sighed and left the gloves on her hands. It shouldn't take her long to go through everything up there and still get to bed before the clock struck one.

Julia grabbed one of the kitchen chairs and placed it as close to the refrigerator as she could, then climbed on top and went to work. She took down a broken water gun that Nicky had asked her to fix last week, a few empty travel mugs that she had forgotten to put away, the mason jar that held all of the matches and lighters, and then she stopped short. Laying next to the mason jar, where it must have been put in a hurry during the hustle and bustle of the day, was the birthday card that Tyler and the kids made for her. Julia took in a sharp breath, then, before she could think her way through it, her eyes filled with tears.

She picked up the card and looked at the happy stick figures on the front next to the giant, lopsided cake. Her fingers trembled. With the card in hand she stepped off the chair and sat down in it sideways so that she was flanked on one side by chair and the other by refrigerator door. Then she cried. Julia sat alone, yellow gloved hands clutching the handmade card, hunched over in the awkwardly placed chair, in the cleanest kitchen she'd had in a while, in her big, beautiful, empty house, and she cried.

It all came flooding back over her, everything. The loneliness when Jim was gone, the first time she met Tyler, drawing him and Sarah playing in the waves, the kid's faces at her surprise birthday party, the bonfire, the song, the night air, the kiss. It all came back through her and she wept, for there was nothing else to do.

She had left the bonfire with determination, knowing that she had to stop this from happening, knowing that it was wrong. She was a mother. She was a *wife* for heaven's sake. All she had to do was cleanse herself, wipe everything clean and start over with Jim. She arranged for Jim's parents to take Randy, Nicky and Sarah for a few days. She vacuumed and dusted and disinfected everything in the house in preparation for Jim coming home tomorrow afternoon.

And now it was midnight, and she felt paralyzed by sadness. An overwhelming hopeless feeling that had been held deep inside for a long time came pouring out in great wracking sobs. And so she wept, until there was nothing left, until she was simply tired. She sniffled, wiped her running nose on the sleeve of the old T-shirt she wore that was reserved for cleaning and painting, took off her gloves, laid them next to the bucket and mop, and carried the card up with her to bed.

The next morning she woke up later than usual. The sun was shining brightly in her bedroom window, gently casting light over the bed and the now semi-crumpled birthday card that was laying on Jim's empty pillow. Julia laid still for a while watching tiny particles float through the sunlight. Then her eyes fell on the birthday card and she knew what she was going to do.

The situation, she figured, was salvageable. They hadn't done anything so terrible, and after sleeping on it she realized that talking it out with Tyler and getting some closure would be good for her, and maybe even for him. She would go over and talk to him today before Jim got home, just to air everything out. She and Tyler could end up friends, which would be nice. There was no reason to make such a Federal case out of the whole situation.

Julia hopped out of bed with fresh enthusiasm. It would

all turn out fine after she had a chance to talk to Tyler. She popped into the master bathroom to brush her teeth and was greeted by a rather worn, puffy reflection. Not only was her hair dirty and a mess, she had slept all night in her grubby cleaning clothes, and all of that crying had left her eyes a little swollen.

"Well," she said to the puffy faced Julia in the mirror, "we can't go talk to him looking like this." As she turned the big knobs on the bathtub and felt the heavy stream of water for its temperature, she wondered if other people talked to themselves when they were alone as much as she seemed to be doing. Half smiling, she retrieved a container of sea salt scrub, the shampoo and conditioner that she purchased at her spa outing just a few weeks ago, and a giant Loofah sponge from the linen closet.

As she sank into the steaming, hot bath she felt good– really good. She would soak in the tub for a while, relax and wash away all of the negativity. Then she would do her hair and make up, and go next door to talk to Tyler before Jim got home this afternoon.

Everything would turn out all right. She would make it all right.

CHAPTER 26

*J*im knew in his heart that he wasn't going home. He had been forced to stay until Saturday because of an important client coming in from Singapore late Friday night. He told his secretary to book him a flight for early Saturday afternoon, so that he could try to make it home for at least part of the weekend, before the real work with the Singaporeans commenced on Monday morning.

But he knew even as he made the request that he would probably come up with an excuse after the Saturday morning breakfast meeting to stay through the weekend. He felt a little bad about it, but it seemed justifiable. How was he supposed to focus on these important business deals while he was flying back and forth and having to handle Julia's emotions? It was too much for him right now.

The company had been represented well with the Singaporeans through breakfast. The CEO and a few other high ups invited him to play racquetball with all of them at the company gym, and he agreed. Jim opted to walk back to the office after the breakfast instead of take a cab with the others, telling them that he had to check in with the wife before joining them for the game.

He took his time walking along the city sidewalk, taking in a few breaths of morning air before the hot, mugginess of August consumed the rest of the day. He didn't know how he was going to tell Julia that he wasn't coming home this weekend. He guessed that she wouldn't say much and that, really, was what he preferred.

This whole thing would have to be fixed. He would talk her down from whatever worries she had worked herself into about moving. He would get her to see that it was best in the long run. After she got into shopping for a house and making the plans, he knew she would be more excited about it all.

However, he really didn't have time to do all of that right now. He had to focus on the merger, on the Singaporeans, on his new position at the company to solidify his future and their future as a family. In time, when Julia looked back at all of this, she would understand that it was for the best. Of that, Jim was certain.

In the meantime his walk was already making him uncomfortably warm, so he removed his cell phone from the inside pocket of his suit jacket and took the jacket off, slinging it over his shoulder as he made his way through the pedestrians and traffic.

He dialed "Jules" on his cell phone and put it to his ear as he walked. That's exactly what he would tell Julia, that he would fix everything when he got home...next week. Until then, she could hang tight and try to enjoy the last few weeks of summer vacation with the kids before it was all over.

CHAPTER 27

*J*ulia stood on the Talvato's doorstep dressed in a white sundress with a bright orange flower print design. She had taken the time to get herself all made up, go to the grocery store to buy supplies for a romantic dinner with Jim, and even stopped at the liquor store for a good bottle of wine. On her way out of the liquor store she saw this dress in the window of one of her favorite boutiques and couldn't resist.

Julia was thrilled to discover that it was even prettier on her than hanging on the mannequin. It hugged her in all the right places and made her feel glamorous. She bought it thinking that Jim would love it, and also knowing that she would wear it when she knocked on Tyler's door to talk things over with him. She couldn't bear the thought of him remembering her as some dowdy Mom. She couldn't bear the thought of him thinking anything bad about her at all.

Now she stood on his doorstep, her stomach full of butterflies. She had rehearsed a small speech that she thought sounded mature. Something about letting things getting out of hand, emotions weren't always controllable, no

135

hard feelings, let's be friends, that kind of thing. As her hand reached up and pushed the doorbell her was heart pounding so hard that she found it difficult to remember the details of her speech.

Her mouth was dry. Her hands were slightly shaking. She felt as if she might throw up. Maybe he wasn't home, she thought to herself, God let him not be home. There was a click as the door unlocked and Julia took in a deep breath, trying to remain calm. The door swung open and Julia froze.

Standing where she was expecting to see Tyler was a young, shapely blonde in a very, very small bikini. Perfectly smooth and tanned, she was strikingly beautiful and stood with an air of annoyance at being disturbed. The smell of coconut suntan lotion and mango perfume drifted over the landing.

"Yes?" The blonde asked, tapping her manicured red nails on the door jam impatiently.

"Is—" Julia found herself stammering, "—i–is Tyler here?"

The blonde's face looked broody, "What do you want?"

Julia was speechless. What did she want? The answers came to her in a rush, none of which she could speak out loud. She wanted to see him again, hear his voice, listen to him laugh, feel him touch her skin, look into his eyes and know that he actually cared about her—mostly, right now, she wanted to disappear off of this porch and out of the sight of this young beauty. Her face was burning hot and she remained utterly mute.

"We don't want any." The blonde said curtly and started to shut the door.

"Wait!" Julia realized that she had spoken too loud. The blonde glowered at her from the half closed door, "I'm the neighbor." She motioned towards her house as if that was proof enough that she wasn't a door-to-door salesperson.

The blonde didn't look at where Julia was pointing. She

didn't care enough. "I'm Julia, the neighbor. I–I should have called." She automatically felt for her cell phone in her pocket, but her new dress had no pockets and she realized that she'd left her phone in her purse all morning. What did that matter anyway? She wasn't thinking straight and knew that she appeared to be a fumbling, tongue-tied, weirdo to the blonde. "Can you just tell Tyler I came by? When he gets back?"

The blonde said something Julia couldn't hear because the door was shutting as she spoke. Her heart was pounding in her ears. She felt dizzy, hot, confused. She turned around and made her way back to her own house as quickly as she could, hoping that none of the neighbors had seen her make such a fool of herself.

CHAPTER 28

$\mathcal{T}$he storm rolled in late afternoon and was still in full force as dark fell over the strip mall. Tyler stood in the large, saloon like window of Rudy's Lounge and looked out at the heavy rain and lightening through the back side of a neon sign for Budweiser beer. He was sipping ice water. After two mornings waking up with a screaming hangover, Tyler had decided to hang out at Rudy's, but curb his drinking. Now that he was watching the storm rage outside he was glad of that. No sense trying to drive home in this nasty weather after having one too many.

The thing was, without liquor to numb his senses, hanging out at Rudy's Lounge was pretty pathetic. Not much to do except reminisce with Samuel, Norene and a few of the other regulars. Even though Tyler had been coming here for less than a week, he'd already heard them repeat more than one sad story. He figured that maybe he could handle being at the Talvato's now. Besides, it was Saturday night and Jim would probably be home. Tyler knew that he and Julia were capable of staying away from each other over the weekend while her husband was around.

Frito trotted up and sat down next to Tyler. He still wore the shredded piece of red bandana that Tyler had tied around his neck for Nicky's pirate party, and after a few months of not getting his normal grooming he had gotten pretty scruffy. Tyler liked him that way. It seemed more natural.

"What do you think, buddy?" Tyler asked the little dog. "Do you think we should go home before this storm gets any worse?" The dog barked in response. Tyler couldn't help but grin. Frito was pretty cool for a dinky rat dog.

Driving back to the Talvato's wasn't too bad, although the rain came down in sheets at times. The lightening was impressive as it lit up the sky enough for him to see the massive, black clouds hanging over the buildings and houses that he passed. Because the storm was so distracting, Tyler didn't take notice of the car parked on the street directly in front of the Talvato's home. He pulled into the driveway, gathered Frito up in his arms to keep him from getting washed away in the torrential rain, and ran to the front door, keys in hand.

A crash of lightening accompanied him as he pushed his way inside the door and into the entryway. The unlit room was momentarily bright with the bluish eerie light that reminded Tyler of many horror movies he had seen. Frito, who had been shivering in his arms until now, started growling ferociously.

"It's all right, buddy. You're gonna be fine." Frito's growling grew more intense and just as Tyler turned on the light switch, he burst into a fit of barking that was fierce for his size.

The sudden light revealed a woman, clad in a flowing black negligee standing on the stairway. Tyler saw her out of the corner of his eye and leapt backwards, almost knocking over one of the strangely erotic statues that sat on a side table near the front door. It took a moment for him to register what he was seeing. It was Tawny.

"Jesus!" Tyler exclaimed.

"Hi, Baby," Tawny spoke seductively as she made her way slowly down the staircase. Frito was writhing in Tyler's arms and barking so loud he could hardly hear Tawny speak. She frowned at the little dog, "What is *that?*"

Tyler, still recovering from the shock, held Frito more firmly in his arms to prevent him from leaping out and lunging at her as she reached the bottom of the staircase.

"*That*," he answered with some derision, "is my dog."

"*You're* dog?" Tawny scoffed at him. "You don't have a dog."

"Tawny," Tyler couldn't talk over the noise Frito was making, so he took a few steps and released the little dog into the back hallway, "Go get a drink, buddy." Frito yipped a few more times then turned quickly and walked away in disgust. Tyler guessed he would probably go to the kitchen and take out his frustration on one of his chew toys.

He turned back around to find Tawny watching him. Now that the commotion was over he was able to take in what she was wearing, which wasn't much. Her long, black, robe was made out of see through netting, as was the bra and panties that she wore underneath. If he looked hard enough, he could see her nipples and the thin strip of hair that she had shaped between her legs whenever she had a bikini wax.

He realized that he was staring and quickly looked up at her face. From her expression he could tell that she had seen him staring. She smiled at him, her lips shining with lip-gloss. Mango, he guessed, that was her favorite.

Tyler ran his hand through his hair in frustration, "Tawny, what are you doing here?"

"What does it look like?" She asked him as she took a few steps in his direction.

"But–but how did you find me? How did you get into the house?" Tyler looked around for an answer to his own question. He was momentarily concerned for the safety of the Talvato's belongings if someone like Tawny could waltz in whenever they felt like it.

"Your Dad arranged it," Tawny answered. Tyler felt the familiar surge of aggravation at the mention of his father. She moved closer, within arms reach of him now. He could smell the Mango on her lips. "Your Dad..." she said sweetly as she reached out and traced her finger up his stomach, "Your Dad really, really supports our relationship, Baby."

Despite the shock of seeing her here, despite the annoyance that his Dad was once again intruding on his life, despite the fact that he was in love with Julia, Tyler found himself aroused by the sleek, blonde beauty standing in front of him. He was working out what to say to her when she stepped forward and kissed him.

He didn't have time to stop her and, in a way, he didn't want to. What man in his right mind would want to stop her? She slipped her hand around his waist and pulled him into her pelvis. The image of her see through panties flashed through his mind. She stopped kissing him for a moment and ran her tongue lightly across his lips then smiled slyly, "You are happy to see me, aren't you?" Before he could answer, her mouth was covering his and her hand was pulling eagerly at the top button of his shorts.

For a few moments Tyler lost himself in the feeling of it all. He felt himself rise towards her hand as it made it's way inside of his shorts. He felt the urgency that always came with Tawny's lovemaking, the almost violent demand that exuded from her. Why not? He asked himself. Why the hell not, it wasn't like he had another girlfriend or anything.

Then he remembered where they were standing, in the well-lit entryway of the Talvato's house, with windows that could be seen not only from the street but from Julia's house as well. Tyler stopped. Tawny felt him freeze and pulled back slightly, "What's the matter, Baby?" He didn't answer and Tawny cocked her head at him, "You don't have another woman hiding around here, do you?"

The question was asked softly enough, but Tyler could feel the antagonism behind the words. Again, he was silent. He didn't have a straight answer, and Tawny wasn't stupid. She pushed herself away from him. He didn't stop her. She gave him a nasty look.

"You're not serious," she said, "where would you find anybody worth fucking up here?" There it was. Tawny's charming personality spilling out, the personality that could ruin the best of moments. "What?" She asked, "Are you banging some high school girl when her parents are at work or something?" Then Tawny gasped. Her eyes opened wide with understanding. She looked at him with surprise and then grim accusation.

Tyler moved away from her and watched her come to some realization that didn't make a lot of sense to him...yet.

"Oh my God," Tawny said. She shook her head with disgust and then laughed out loud in spite of herself. Her eyes narrowed and she looked at him again, "Oh my God, Tyler, you're fucking the desperate housewife that came over today, aren't you? That's why she was so freaked out!"

Tyler was confused, "What are you talking about?" Tawny laughed, harder this time. It wasn't a cheerful sound. It sounded canned and criticizing. "Tawny, who came over today? What do you mean?" Tyler asked again. She didn't answer.

His mind was racing. Was it just his own wishful thinking, or had Julia come by today and found Tawny there instead of him? His heart felt like it was pounding out of his chest. Had she come to him? Why? He looked out into the pouring rain and could barely see the light glowing from her living room window.

He didn't care why. He was sure she had come to see him and he had missed her. He took one look at Tawny sniggering in her negligee and pushed past her.

"Hey–" she shouted at him as he stepped into the storm. He didn't hear the rest of what she said, because he had already slammed the door behind him.

CHAPTER 29

*J*ulia sat curled up in the fat living room chair under a blanket. She had a glass of wine on the table next to her and her wedding album open in her lap. The gloomy night fit her mood perfectly. She was reveling in the sound of rain falling heavily on her roof, water dripping off of the eaves, and the melancholy piano solos of Yiruma playing over and over on repeat in the background.

After the encounter with the Victoria Secret's model Tyler had hidden away with him next door, she returned home feeling old and unattractive, only to find a message from Jim telling her that he was not coming home this weekend.

She gave up on the idea of cooking dinner and broke open the special bottle of wine she had bought earlier in the day. Then the storm started and, too morose to watch a movie, she was instead drawn to the photo albums, her wedding album specifically. Now, over halfway through the bottle of wine, she flipped slowly through the pages looking at the very happy, very young faces. Such a long time ago.

At first she thought the knocking was thunder. She wasn't expecting anyone so when she heard it again, a solid thumping on her front door, she considered ignoring it. Then she decided that just because her world was falling down around her didn't mean she had to leave some delivery guy standing outside in this weather. She left her wine and her wedding album on the table in the living room, wrapped her blanket around her shoulders, and went to see who was there.

When she opened the door, time simply stopped. Tyler, his hands self-consciously shoved into his pockets, his clothes soaking wet, his hair a mass of dark, dripping curls, was standing on her front porch. She stood there, looking at him for a long moment, taking in every detail of him, as if he wasn't real.

"Julia," his voice choked slightly, but the sound of him saying her name sent a thrill down her spine. "Sorry to bother you guys."

The spell was broken, "You're soaking wet," she said and ushered him into the house. He came inside the door and she closed it to the sound of distant thunder rumbling.

When she turned to him, he hadn't moved much past her, perhaps trying not to drip water all over her floor, perhaps not wanting to leave her side. It didn't matter because she found herself just inches away from him. He looked at her intently, his deep brown eyes soft and sad. He hadn't shaved in a few days and the 5 o'clock shadow did nothing but make him even more ruggedly handsome. The thrill traveled down her spine again.

"I didn't know if I should come by so late—if I would wake up the kids." Tyler glanced into the house for signs of the children...or Jim.

"They're not here," Julia informed him, then, "Jim's not here either." Tyler's eyebrows raised in surprise. Julia tried to ignore his questioning gaze by fussing, "What are you doing out in the rain?" She took the blanket from her own shoulders and wrapped it around his and, by doing so, moved even closer to him. Tyler watched her evenly as she did this, taking his hands out of his pockets in order to grab the blanket and keep it from dropping onto the floor. Her hands shook slightly as she brushed against his wet shirt, "I mean, you're absolutely soaked to the bone!"

"Julia," Tyler said, taking her hands into his, Julia noticed that his hands were trembling also, "Did you come to see me today?"

Julia looked straight into his eyes, "Yes. Yes I did—and I met your—your girlfriend." She felt jealousy flare up in her voice and tried to pull away from him, but he was holding her hands tightly.

"Ex, she's my ex-girlfriend and I didn't know she was here. I didn't know until I got home tonight." He was apologizing. She felt embarrassed because she was acting like she had some claim on him. Tyler continued to hold her hands, his eyes locked onto hers, "Why did you come over?"

"I don't know—I wanted to talk to—I think we should—" she fumbled for the words, then sighed. It was no use. Her words were gone. The only thing she could think about was how happy she was that he was standing there next to her. "I had a speech and everything," she told him.

He broke into his irresistible dimpled smile, "Oh yeah? A speech?" She nodded then giggled at his teasing. Tyler's eyes twinkled at her and wandered up and down her body, taking in her new dress that she had left on in an attempt to keep herself cheerful. "You look beautiful," he told her, then his brow furrowed in concern, "You must be cold. Here," he quickly took the blanket she had given him and swept it around the both of them so they were in an upright cocoon, "There," he said.

Julia let him pull her close to him, feeling the warmth of his body underneath his wet clothes, "Now we're both going to be soaked!" She protested.

"No," he answered as he wrapped his arms even more securely around her and leaned down so their lips were almost touching, "Now we're both going to be warm."

~

They didn't decide to go to bed. There was no thinking about it or talking it through. When Julia went over it many years later in her mind the explanation was simple–they belonged together. Laying naked under the covers with Tyler as the rain fell on the roof and the thunder rolled in the distance wasn't something she chose to do, she didn't make a decision to do it, she just let go and didn't try to stop it anymore.

He was perfect. That was all. He kissed her and she fell into a place that she'd never been before, a place where their bodies melded, their fingers entwined, and their souls seemed to dance. There was no need to speak, but Tyler whispered to her as he moved on top of her. He whispered into her neck, into her ear, and into her chest as he kissed her gently. He stroked her breasts and took her nipple softly into his mouth. Pure pleasure flowed through her body and she arched her back, pushing herself into him.

His response was visceral. Every muscle in his body tightened, but his touch remained sweet and calm. As he rolled his tongue over her nipple, adding to her excitement, his hand slid down her stomach, circled over her thigh and slipped between her legs. The tingling sensation that his touch always brought to her was magnified a hundred times and she felt a surge of desire so strong that her whole abdomen constricted. She moaned and her fingers, which had been caressing his taunt back, now grabbed onto him. She felt his finger push inside her and knew that he would find the hot, wetness that he was seeking, and he did.

It was immediate, the moment his finger pushed into her, the exact pressure of his hand, the weight of his hard body on hers, the smell of him, the way the muscles on his shoulders were flexing as his hand moved between her legs, all brought her to orgasm. She tensed, she pulled him closer to her pulsing body, she cried out and felt the rush of heat flow between her legs and over his hand.

Then he was on top of her, his mouth covering hers, his knees pushing her legs wider apart. She was still coming when he slid inside of her, so thick, so hard inside of her that the feel of him added to her gratification and she cried out again, the heat between her legs rising to an impossible crescendo. He stopped kissing her and lifted his torso up slightly so he could look into her eyes. They moved together that way, gazing into each other's eyes, her fingers running through his hair and across his chest as he thrust into her again and again, until her pleasure was spent.

When she was calm, Tyler leaned down and kissed her, then, shaking his head in amazement he whispered "God, Julia" She smiled at him and slid her hand to the back of his neck, pulling his mouth to hers. She tasted him, slipping her tongue inside of his lips, delighting in the way he felt. She could feel his body tighten and knew that he was ready. At first he moved slowly, then faster and faster, driving his hardness into her, she matched him each time, gripping the back of his neck, keeping his mouth on hers, opening herself to his tongue, to his whole body.

Then he came with such power inside of her she thought he might cry out like she had, but he didn't. Instead he embraced her tightly and dropped his mouth into her neck as he released all of himself into her. She held him close, feeling his ragged breath on her skin and the pounding of his heart on her naked breast.

When it was over it felt like the most natural thing in the world to be nestled in his arms, listening to the rain that was falling more softly now, the storm was past. Julia's cheek lay on his chest and she could feel the soft beating of his heart. She played with his chest hair and let her fingers drift across his perfect abs.

They didn't sleep right away. They talked long into the night. He told her about Austin and his musician friends who were waiting for him there, waiting to make it big. She told him memories she had of art class in college and the group of crazy friends she had known back then that had since dispersed into their various adult lives. They talked about big rain storms that frightened and thrilled them as children, about their families, about their favorite songs, about the things that made them laugh and cry.

Finally they both drifted to sleep and woke in the morning to the delight of finding each other still there. It only took moments for their desire to take over and they made love once more. With less urgency and more knowledge of each other, Julia found herself reaching levels of ecstasy that she had never experienced with Jim or anyone else in her past. All she wanted to do was stay wrapped in Tyler's arms and rest a while so they could do it again before getting out of bed.

She told Tyler what she was thinking and he laughed, "That," he kissed her forehead, her cheek and then her mouth, "is the best idea I've heard in a while."

"You don't think I sound just a bit like a sex maniac?" She asked him, only half kidding.

"No," he chuckled, "actually, you sound like the woman of my dreams!" They both laughed at that and snuggled closer. "In fact," he continued his thought, "my life would be perfect if you would only come to Austin with me in September."

Julia's first reaction was absolute delight. Imagine a life with Tyler, her hunky, fun loving, guitar playing Tyler, in Austin. She would get back into art, he would play in bars at night, they would spend hours every night making love, wrapped in each other's arms.

Then, of course, reality filtered into Julia's thoughts, and she felt a great sadness come over her. She was only free until tomorrow afternoon, when Jim's parents brought the kids back home. She turned over so that she was laying on her stomach next to him, and propped herself up on her elbows. She didn't want to think about all of that right now. She only wanted to think about him. He smiled at her. She smiled back and started to speak, "Tyler, I want you to know that--"

Her cell phone started buzzing on the nightstand next to her. She looked at him apologetically, "The kids are with their grandparents. I should get that." He nodded in agreement and she grabbed her phone. The number showing was not one that her phone recognized, but it wasn't a 1-800 number so it probably wasn't a salesman. She answered it.

"Hello?"

"Mrs. Fischer?"

"Yes," Something about the woman's voice gave Julia the feeling of an invisible, clammy hand wrapping around her neck.

"This is Charlotte Memorial Hospital, there's been an accident."

The walls, doorways and signs in the wide hospital hallway all blurred together. At least it seemed that way to Julia, who could only focus on the woman, donned in hospital green, who walked in front of them, showing them the way to the ICU. She was aware of Tyler following just behind her to her right, but only just. Everything was dimmed except the woman in green, walking briskly through an elaborate hallway system that seemed, to Julia, to be impossibly long.

Then suddenly the hallway opened up into a yellowish waiting area and there was Ed and Tracy turning towards her, eyes swollen, looking older than they had a few days ago when they drove away with all of the kids strapped safely in the backseat of their car. Tracy was holding Sarah, who was fast asleep.

They all stood up and walked to meet Julia. It seemed like slow motion until Randy's arms wrapped around her waist and she felt his face hot against her stomach. She hugged him tightly and put her cheek into his uncombed hair. He stammered something she couldn't understand, she merely answered, "It's okay, honey, it's okay."

Then the green lady was speaking, "Mrs. Fischer, you can come with me. The Doctor will be coming in to check on Nicholas, he'll want to talk to you." Julia nodded. She kissed the top of Randy's head and laid her hand on Sarah's back.

Ed put out his hand, so much like Jim's, and laid it on her shoulder. With only a cursory glance towards Tyler, he said, "You go on in. We'll look after the children and keep an eye out for Jim."

Julia nodded again. She started to speak but was lost for words. She looked for only a brief second at Tyler, who was standing a few steps to the side of her in-laws. He would wait for her, she knew. He gave her a quick nod then she turned around and followed the green lady down the hall.

For the first few moments after she walked into the ICU it appeared that the bed the nurse was ushering her towards was empty. She realized quickly that this was because she could only see the foot of the bed, which was made for adults, and after taking a few steps closer to it Nicky's feet were plainly visible under the thin, white, hospital blankets. His tiny body barely made a bump in that big bed. But during those few moments, those few steps where the bed seemed to be empty, the clammy hand that had kept it's grip around her neck for the entire ride to the hospital, moved instantly to her heart and turned to ice.

Except for the coldness surrounding her heart, Julia was numb as she approached the side of the hospital bed where her youngest son lay attached to a variety of tubes and machines. The left side of his face was so swollen that his eye couldn't have opened, even if he'd been conscious. There were four long, black lines of stitches on the left side of his face, about two or three inches long, and a splint that covered his entire left arm. His breathing was very shallow, and he looked terribly pale. However, the beeping of one of the machines attached to him assured her that his heart was beating. Julia held onto that sound with her entire soul.

She didn't know how long she stayed at Nicky's bedside. A different nurse, not the green lady, but one dressed in pale mauve, moved a chair around so that she could sit down. Then Julia sat there, watching her son breathe, stroking his hand, his arm, his hair, without knowing how much time was passing.

The Doctor came in at one point. He was very tall and lanky, with short brown hair and long hands. He seemed a little young to Julia. He introduced himself to her, but she immediately forgot his name. He explained what had happened to her son, the injuries that the impact from the car had inflicted. He talked about each injury separately, giving her details on the level of seriousness and recovery expectations.

As he spoke Julia could only pick out certain words and

phrases, like "multiple fractures", "contusions", "brain damage". The room that surrounded the Doctor grew black. She could no longer hear the words he was saying even though she could see his mouth moving. There was a buzzing noise that kept getting louder and louder. Then she heard a man's voice, "We're losing her," and everything went black.

CHAPTER 30

*W*hen Jim was buckled safely into his airplane seat, waiting to taxi out onto the runway and take off, he thought time couldn't move any slower. That was true, until now. He was currently stuck in a cab behind some ridiculous traffic jam that seemed to be caused by a large crowd leaving a baseball game. He felt like he was in some strange, science fiction movie where everyone around him was trapped in a dull dream state. Nothing, absolutely nothing, anyone did was fast enough for him, nor could it get him to his family as quickly as it should. Adding salt to the wound was the idea that had been gnawing at him during his whole flight—he should have been home yesterday.

He felt like screaming at the cab driver and anyone else that came into his path. They all seemed to sense it, eyeing him sideways and watching to make sure he wasn't a lunatic carrying a bomb. He was sure that if he looked as desperate or as sick with worry as he felt, he probably did look like a lunatic. They were smart to stay out of his way.

Jim took in a deep breath in an attempt to calm down.

Even the air had slowed to a crawl and it took him far too long to fill his lungs. Nicky's condition was serious, very serious, and he was getting insufficient details from Julia and his folks to ease his mind. His Mom was useless during crisis, always had been. Julia was unavailable. As far as he could determine she was spending most of her time at Nicky's side. His Dad, thank goodness, was more helpful and, in his own way, was holding down the fort until Jim could get there.

Jim looked at his watch, something he'd done countless times since he got Julia's panicked phone call this morning. He hoped that he would never have to hear her like that again. The frantic sound in her voice, her obvious confusion, borderline hysteria, and the fact that she kept apologizing over and over was strange. In all the years they had been together, Jim had never heard her so distraught. The fact that she must handle this all by herself worried him. He didn't want her to be alone.

She had caught him getting ready to play another game of racquetball with the Singapore crowd. It was shocking to hear her like that and he wasn't sure if he'd made the circumstances clear to the company men before he ran out the door. That didn't matter. He needed to be with Julia, he needed to be with Nicky, he needed to be with his family.

The taxi stopped again, and Jim decided that he would get out and run the rest of the way. He simply could not sit here one minute longer. Jim grabbed the handle and started to say as much to the cabbie when he looked up and realized that it was unnecessary. They were stopped at the hospital entrance.

In the waiting room Jim found his parents and Tyler with Randy and Sarah. Tyler must have come to help babysit, he was sitting on the floor with Sarah in the section of the waiting room that the hospital had set up for children. Randy sat near them and stood up when Jim entered the room. Jim went to his oldest son and wrapped his arm protectively around his shoulders as his own father and mother explained what had happened.

Nicky had gotten up early, as usual, and eaten breakfast before any of them were awake. He had poked his head into his Grandparent's bedroom to ask if he could go outside and ride his bike in the driveway. At this part of the story, Jim's mother began to cry softly. His father cleared his throat and continued, "Son, I told him he had to put on his helmet and to stay in the driveway. I told him he couldn't go in the street until I came outside."

The rest of the story Jim could guess, but he let them tell him anyway. Nicky hadn't done what he was told. He had rode his bike into the street and a few minutes later, as his Dad was getting a cup of coffee and Randy was wandering into the kitchen to get a bowl of cereal, they heard the screeching of tires and a sickening thud. They heard the woman who was driving the car start screaming even before they could get out the front door.

"Is Julia with him?" Jim asked, his voice gruff, his arm still holding Randy firmly.

"Yes," his father answered.

Jim turned to speak to Randy, "I'm going to be with Mom and Nicky for a little bit," Randy nodded, "I'll check on everything Randy," he tousled his son's hair, "don't worry." Jim looked towards Sarah in the play area.

Tyler had picked her up and moved closer to the conversation. Sarah was busy bopping him on the side of the head with a Nerf ball. Jim stepped towards them and reached out to take his daughter for a few moments before he had to leave. Sarah pulled back from him and buried her face shyly into Tyler's shoulder.

A strange feeling shot through Jim. He looked at the young man who was holding his daughter. Tyler didn't look back at him, he busied himself trying to extract Sarah's little hand from the tight grip it had on his shirt, "Look, Sarah, your Dad's here."

"No!" Sarah exclaimed. She threw the Nerf ball towards Jim and held on to Tyler with both hands now.

Jim's hands remained extended towards his daughter, but his eyes were fixed on Tyler. There was something strange about how he was acting. The guy was much too embarrassed for the circumstances. It was just an overtired baby girl after all, nothing too surprising about that. There was something else in Tyler's demeanor that captured his attention, something that didn't fit.

Jim was a smart man. He hadn't made it to the levels that he had reached in the world of finance without being able to read another man's body language. And Tyler, the college kid from next door, the babysitter, the guy that had been, according to his wife, hanging out at Jim's house over the summer, giving guitar lessons to Randy, roughhousing with Nicky in the swimming pool, accompanying his whole family to the beach, baking birthday cakes for Julia and giving her gifts, that same young man was giving off a confusing vibe. He seemed...guilty. What did Tyler have to feel guilty about?

"Jim?" It was Julia's voice, coming from behind him. In the instant before he heard his name he could see Tyler look past him, and Jim watched the young man's expression transform from guilt to something entirely different, something sad and unprotected. He turned from Tyler towards the sound of his wife's voice, a feeling of doubt remaining at the edge of his mind.

The air felt thick around him, even thicker than before in the airplane and the cab. Jim had difficulty moving through it. It was like he had finally been sucked into the slow motion nightmare that he'd been watching all day as he tried to find his way to the bedside of his injured son.

When Jim saw Julia his heart sunk. She stood in the fluorescent light of the yellow waiting room, her shoulders slumped, barely keeping her balance. Her eyes had large circles under them and she was pale. So pale and unsteady that he thought she must be about to faint. His instincts kicked in and he rushed to her side. He caught her hand in his and placed his arm around her shoulders. She felt light, as if with the slightest push she would just topple over or crumple to the ground right where she stood.

The strange feeling that Jim had felt emanating from Tyler was forgotten. He couldn't think about anything except Julia and Nicky now. He pulled his wife to him and held her close. Her skin was cool, and he thought that she probably needed to lay down and rest. She must be exhausted.

He kissed the top of her head and held her more tightly, "It's going be all right, Jules." He could feel rather than hear her crying. Her shoulders softly shaking in his arms, her tears hot and wet soaking through his shirt. He stood there supporting his wife while she wept, a sickening feeling of grief and anxiety rising through his body.

When she was able to lead him to Nicky's room, he followed. Leaving behind his worried parents, Sarah crying for her Mother in Tyler's arms, and Randy watching everything with a stoic resolve that surprised Jim. Randy, he thought as he left the waiting room behind, was a pretty great kid.

The sight of Nicky laying mute and bandaged in his hospital bed was impossible. He found himself breathing deeply, in and out, in an attempt to control his emotions. He didn't know what would happen if he let them go. He didn't know if he was going to scream or drop onto the floor crying

or rage like some kind of a wild bull, knocking over equip-
ment and crashing through doors.

So he kept as still as he could, breathing in and breathing
out, one hand on Julia's back, one hand touching Nicky's
arm, as Julia stroked their son's face and spoke quietly to
him, just like she used to do when he was a baby and he
couldn't go to sleep.

CHAPTER 31

*A*fter Julia and Jim had left to see Nicky, it was decided that Ed and Tracy would take Sarah back to their house with them. A hospital waiting room was no place for a baby. Randy was adamant about staying near his parents, so Tyler offered to sit with him in the waiting room. He hoped that Jim's parents took the gesture as him doing something nice for the whole family, instead of what it really was, an attempt to stay as close to Julia as possible.

Seeing her so upset was almost more than Tyler could take. There was nothing he could do for her, no way he could walk over and comfort her the way Jim had done. What he was feeling was more than jealousy. It was a profound yearning that took everything in his power to control. All he could do was stand and watch as Julia held tightly to her husband and wept.

After everyone was gone, Tyler took Randy down to the cafeteria to get something to eat. It took a little convincing, but in the end Randy decided that a ten minute walk down to the cafeteria and back didn't mean the end of the world.

It was a quiet walk. Neither of them felt much like talking, but Tyler thought it was good that Randy ate most of the peanut butter and jelly sandwich and bag of chips he bought him. The sight of food made Tyler sick, so he just got a cup of coffee and a bagel and cream cheese in a bag to take back to the waiting room. He figured Randy might get hungry later, and a bagel was better than a candy bar at the vending machine.

They waited there for what felt like an eternity. Randy sunk deeper and deeper into his chair. He refused any offers Tyler made of magazines to look at and even chose not to play games on Tyler's phone. After a while, Tyler stopped trying to distract the kid and they both just sat there, staring.

He knew that Julia was a mess, that Jim and Randy were there for her, and that he didn't really belong here, but he didn't know what to do. Every time his mind wandered away from the sickening fact that Nicky was laying so badly hurt in the other room, that Randy was sitting there next to him reliving every moment of finding his little brother crushed under a car, and that he had spent the night before with their Mom, Tyler's mind would kind of trip out.

The images of her in bed pushed their way into his thoughts and he knew that he had to be some kind of sick son-of-a-bitch to have sex fantasies in the middle of the hospital, in the middle of this crazy situation. There was nothing he could do to stop the memories. Her skin, her touch, her smell, Christ, her scent was still on him.

Tyler stood up abruptly and began to pace across the floor of the waiting room. Randy watched him, brooding.

What was he going to do when Julia returned? Was he going to offer to drive her home? Were they going to tell Jim? Would he have a chance to be alone with her? What was he thinking? Nicky was the only thing that was important right now, getting Nicky back to normal. He had to stop thinking about himself.

Tyler ran his hand through his hair, like he always did when he was nervous or confused, making it stand up on end. He realized that he probably looked crazy. He'd dressed so quickly after Julia got the news about Nicky, he didn't even notice what he'd put on. With a quick glance down, Tyler felt some relief that at least he'd put his clothes on in some kind of order, his shirt wasn't on backwards or anything. Randy was watching him and Tyler suddenly felt ashamed.

"Hey, sport," he gave Randy what he thought was a reassuring smile and took a seat next to him again, "How are you holding up?" Randy shrugged. "You want to go home for a little bit?" Randy shook his head "no". Tyler nodded in agreement. More silence.

He didn't know why he said what he said next. As he spoke the words he couldn't be sure if he was trying to comfort Randy or himself, but they just kind of spilled out of his mouth, there was no taking it back. "You know, sport, it's not your fault." Randy stiffened. "There's no reason to feel guilty or anything like that. You couldn't have known this would happen, nobody could. Sometimes things happen and someone gets hurt and you can't feel bad about it..." Tyler would have kept talking but he was stopped by the expression on Randy's face.

The little boy's chin started quivering, his face flushed, and his hands gripped the arms of the chair he was sitting in. He looked at Tyler with narrowed eyes that were dangerously close to tears and what Tyler saw wasn't grief or fear or guilt. He saw anger, "You're not my Dad." That's all Randy said, four little words–four words that shot right through him.

He fumbled for an answer, "I–Ran–", Randy didn't let him finish.

"You keep acting like my Dad, and you're not my Dad."

Tyler couldn't say anything. What was there to say? He was right. He was not and could never be his Dad. He wasn't anything worthwhile to any of them. Tyler tried to say something that would reassure the boy, but whatever words he thought he was going to say got stuck in his throat. Instead of explaining himself, or offering wisdom or comfort to the kid, Tyler swallowed hard and looked down at his own hands.

Randy must have taken pity on him, because after a few moments he laid his small hand on top of Tyler's. Tyler looked at the boy and was unable to mask his sadness. The anger had dissipated from Randy's face, and he peered into Tyler's eyes , "You're a cool guy. We all like you, but you're just not our Dad."

Tyler understood. It was nothing but the truth, and it had taken a child to point it out.

CHAPTER 32

*I*n the week that Nicky was in the hospital he grew stronger and, due to the excellent care and skill of his surgeons, he was on the mend. Julia was never able to bring herself to leave the building, preferring to keep a constant vigil so that she could be there when he became conscious. Even with the nursing staff checking in on him, she didn't want to take the chance of him waking up and being alone.

Her dedication was rewarded when on the third night, sometime around 2:30 in the morning, Nicky finally opened his eyes and spoke to her. He was dulled down and foggy from medication and from the mere effort of fighting back from his injuries, but he knew who she was and Julia wept with relief. After he fell back asleep, she called Jim who had gone home to be with Randy and Sarah, and told him. They wept together.

Jim had been wonderful. He stayed busy running between their house, his parent's house and the hospital, managing everyone and making sure that Julia could stay uninterrupted with her youngest son. He knew she couldn't bear the thought of leaving Nicky, and he was 100% supportive. If devotion was enough to cure someone, he told her, then he was sure Nicky would be just fine.

They hadn't spoken much, really, in that week, but having him there with her and at home with their other children, eased her mind. Most of the time, when she stood or sat at Nicky's bedside, Jim positioned himself just behind her and to her left, and his physical presence made her feel reassured. It had been such a long time since she felt like Jim was really with her, and it made her both happy and sad. Happy that he was there, sad that it had taken this terrible crisis for him to come back to her side, and sadder still when she let her thoughts turn towards Tyler.

He had stayed at the hospital, waiting, for much of the first day. Waiting for what, she couldn't say. Waiting for news on Nicky, waiting for her, she couldn't be sure. She had barely spoken to him during the car ride to the hospital, and barely looked at him after they arrived, and she had barely thought of him for the first few days except for an occasional stabbing of regret. Regret for how she had betrayed her husband, regret for the moments she was laying in Tyler's arms when her son was laying battered in the street, and regret that she had caused, or would cause, any of them pain, Tyler included.

Julia looked across Nicky's sleeping form at her husband. This afternoon, for some reason, Jim wasn't sitting next to her, but on the opposite side of Nicky's bed. Both he and his son were dozing, Nicky comfortably resting in his bed, and Jim sitting sideways in the hospital chair, awkwardly resting his head on his hand. Julia smiled at his crumpled clothes. He looked worn out and uncomfortable and nothing like he did when he was in his high-powered business suit. He looked more like he used to when they were in college.

Julia watched her husband and son sleep until the technician came in to roll Nicky down the hallway to get some new X-Rays. He was scheduled to have surgery the next morning and the surgeon had requested new films. The technician told Julia that Nicky was not likely to wake up during the procedure, as he'd had a mild sedative and they could do what they needed to do without disturbing him too much. She suggested that the tired parents wait for her in the room, and then she pulled Nicky, bed and all, out the door.

Julia noted that with the bed gone there was a giant space left between her and Jim. She looked up at him from staring at the floor. He was awake now, running his hands up and down the stubble on his cheeks in an attempt to stay that way. He yawned and stretched his arms out to the side. Noticing Julia watching him he shook his head, "Man, I cannot wake up. I don't know how you've been doing it, Jules."

She smiled quietly. She didn't want to tell him that she'd been kept awake for days by fear, dread, guilt, and the kind of adrenalin that comes from your world crashing down around you. Instead she said, "You should go get a cup of coffee or something from the cafeteria."

"No," he shook his head, "I'll be all right." He was sitting with his feet set wide apart and he leaned forward, resting his elbows on his knees, "Do you want some coffee?"

She shook her head, "No, thanks."

That was it. That was the extent of their conversation for a long while. Julia, despite herself, found her mind wandering to Tyler, wondering what he was doing, remembering the feel of his skin against hers, wishing she could talk with him, knowing that she couldn't. Lost in her own thoughts, Julia's expression had fallen and she was hunched over in her chair, staring at the great empty floor in front of her. Jim was watching her.

"Julia?" He hardly ever used her full name. She looked up. His eyes were worn and red rimmed from losing too much sleep, "Julia, I think we should talk."

CHAPTER 33

The weather had begun to fail. A thick haze muted the clouds so that their normal glowing white seemed grey and matched the rest of the sky. The frothy peaks of the waves looked almost like snow until they rolled closer and melted over the black rocks jutting up from an outcropping that stretched into the water.

Tyler was perched on a large black rock that sat farther back, away from the water. It had been cold enough for him to wear jeans and a dark blue hoodie to the beach today. He didn't mind. The weather wasn't going to stop him from coming here. In fact, he liked it even more when the chill kept other people away.

Frito raced back to him, carrying his tiny, yellow squeaky ball that Nicky had named Bean Ball in his mouth and dropping it into Tyler's hand. "Thanks, Frito," Tyler praised him as he drew his arm back and threw the ball down the beach. Frito raced after it, barking happily.

It was almost a week since he'd seen or talked to Julia. He left the hospital that first day, when Randy's grandfather returned to check on them and hadn't gone back.

Since then, he and Frito spent all of their time either at the beach or at Rudy's Lounge. Tyler didn't have the heart to stay at the Talvato's, watching out the window for Julia or a sign of what was going on with Nicky. He left early enough and came home late enough to make sure there was no chance he might run into Julia, Randy, Jim...any of them. He hoped Nicky was all right, but he knew it wasn't his place to find out.

And then yesterday he got the text, "Nicky is okay. Meet me at the bonfire tomorrow at 3pm. I would like to talk." That's all it said, nothing huge, no declarations of love, no warnings to stay away, just a few sentences to let him know that Nicky was going to be fine and that she wanted to talk to him. Yet those few sentences sent him reeling.

He'd been sitting on this same rock watching Frito chase seagulls when he read it. His stomach clenched when he saw it was from her, and as he read the words he felt relief for Nicky and elation that she wanted to see him. His joy was quickly followed by uneasiness over the last words, "I would like to talk." They sounded ominous, but he didn't care. He would see her. That's all that mattered.

Right on time, Julia appeared on the beach about twenty yards away from him. She wore a white T-shirt with a jean jacket, and a long, rose print skirt that flapped lightly around her legs from the combination of her motion and the wind. She had pulled her hair back in a loose ponytail and pieces of it were lifted by the wind and blew gently around her face. Tyler's heart caught in his chest when he saw her. For a few moments he watched her walk along the sand towards him. He was frozen in place, watching her move through the sand and the breeze, with the sky and the land and the water blending around her like it was all a dream, and then she smiled.

Tyler stood up and walked, then jogged, to meet her. She started to say something to greet him, but he scooped her into his arms and held on to her, feeling her hold on to him just as tightly. They stayed this way without a word. Holding her like this he wasn't sure he would be capable of letting her go, but after a few minutes he felt her let go of him, gently, and he knew, for the last time.

"Tyler," she said, and the sound of her speaking his name filled him with pain.

"Nicky's okay?" He interrupted. He didn't want to know what she was about to say.

"Yes," Julia's face brightened at the thought, "He's pulled through everything. They say he can come home soon, and in a few months he'll be completely back to normal."

The word 'normal' hung in the air for a few moments then Julia gave him an "oh, no" face.

"You'll have your hands full!" Tyler joked. They both chuckled at the idea of Nicky's normal, crazy self, and any tension between them was gone. Tyler grabbed her hand and squeezed it, as always unable to keep himself from touching her. He lifted her hand to his lips and kissed it warmly, "He's a great kid." He was surprised to hear his own voice break as he spoke. There was a hot, tightening in his throat and he couldn't say anything else. He kissed her hand again, and quickly brushed a tear from his eye.

Julia took both of his hands in hers, "Tyler--"

He nodded quickly, "I know," He breathed in and out, trying hard not to cry. The heat in his throat was in his gut now, a hard ball centered right below his stomach, he felt sick.

"I'm sorry," she said, and lifted his hands to her cheek. She held them there for a long time. He could feel her tears soft on his skin. Then she took a deep breath, pulled back and looked into his eyes, her own hazel eyes shone from being wet, "No," she said, "I'm not sorry. I won't ever be sorry." She pulled his hands to her lips and brushed them with a kiss, then dropped them down and let go.

Tyler watched as she put her hands in the pockets of her jean jacket. He nodded in agreement, "Neither will I."

Julia smiled, "So, have you decided to go to Austin when you leave?"

Tyler shoved his hands into the pouch on the front of his hoodie and looked out over the water for a moment, contemplating. Then he turned to her, taking in every feature of her face for the last time, and grinned, "Yeah, why not?"

From his vantage point in the upstairs music room of the Talvato's house, Tyler could see the black SUV pull into her driveway. He watched as Julia got Sarah out of her car seat and Jim retrieved Nicky from the back seat, carrying him easily towards the front door. Tyler could see that Nicky was talking incessantly. He was holding three small red Nerf balls and threw them, one-by-one, at his big brother who was walking a few paces behind them.

Without being able to hear them, he knew that it was chaos. That Sarah was babbling and squealing, that Randy was doing his best to help with the other kids, that Julia was answering a stream of questions from Nicky, that it was a boisterous, disorderly, bumbling family.

Jim pretended to trip on the stairs and held Nicky out over the bushes as if he was going to drop him. Nicky's face, even though it was pale and thin, filled with delight at his father's joke. Tyler watched as Julia first scolded Jim and then laughed with all of them. She held the door open and Jim gave her a quick kiss as he walked past her with their son. She beamed at her husband. Tyler turned away from the window.

His duffle bag and guitar waited for him near the door. Frito sat expectantly next to the baggage, wagging his tail and holding Bean Ball in his mouth. The Talvato's were expected in less than five hours, and Tyler had decided to take off before they got here. He wasn't in the mood to make small talk, but he was a little worried about Frito.

"Hey, buddy," he said to the little dog as he picked him up and scratched the scruff of his neck, "I'm gonna head out. Your people will be back tonight." Frito dropped Bean Ball into Tyler's hand and began happily wiggling and licking his chin. Tyler put Frito on the carpet and threw Bean Ball down the hallway for him. He picked up his duffle bag and guitar and made his way down the steps to the front door.

Frito raced to the front door squeaking Bean Ball in his mouth the whole time, ready for another adventure. Tyler put his hand on the door handle and said, "Frito, you can't come with me today. You have to stay here." The little dog's ears drooped and he let the squeaky toy fall to the floor. "I'm sorry, buddy." Frito whimpered.

Tyler carefully opened the door enough to get his luggage outside without leaving room for Frito to escape. When he turned to close and lock the door he saw that there was no need for him to do that. Frito had curled up in a tiny ball in the center of the huge entryway and was watching him with doleful eyes. He whimpered again.

Tyler took a look around the giant, gaudily decorated space and then back to the scruffy little dog that had once been a nippy, pedigreed, pain in the ass. He thought about it for a split second, and then he opened the door wide, "All right," he said. Frito's head perked up, "Come on." Frito yipped happily and ran full speed out the front door, "Don't forget Bean Ball," Tyler told him. The little dog made a 180-degree turn and raced back into the house, noisily grabbing the squeaky toy and carried it out with him.

"My Dad's gonna kill me," Tyler told Frito. Then he locked the door and left.

CHAPTER 34

*S*arah sat in the back seat of the car, still too small to sit in the passenger side next to her Mom, but big enough to peer out the window and watch the sights go by on her way to start school. She had chosen a pink and grey checked sundress, pink sweater, and white sandals to wear for her first day of Kindergarten. She asked Julia to braid her hair and, as Jim said earlier in the morning when they took her First Day of School picture, she looked like a princess.

Julia looked at her daughter in the rear view mirror, "What do you think is the most exciting part about going to school?"

Sarah, who could be a quiet and serious minded little thing, thought about it for a moment and then said, "Miss Samantha."

"Oh, you're excited to spend the day with Miss Samantha?"

Sarah nodded, "Yes, she's nice and she has big, curly hair."

Julia laughed, "Yes, she does. You're going to have a wonderful time, sweetie."

The poignancy of taking her youngest child to her first

day of school wasn't lost on Julia. The whole family had been involved in this most special morning. The boys encouraged her and fussed over her and Julia got the feeling they were more worried about their little sister than her own parents. Jim made pancakes while Julia helped Sarah get dressed and they all celebrated the morning together. It was fun and exciting and good.

Jim took the boys to drop them off at their first day of classes, which started earlier, on his way to work. And now Julia was driving Sarah. They arrived at the school and found Miss Samantha. Julia watched her baby step into the world of being a "big girl" and felt proud, excited and sad all at once. Then, like everything in life, the moment was over. The bell rang, school began, and Julia was back in her car heading to her art class.

She had started drawing classes at a local art college part-time last year, after exhausting all of the best books she could find on the subject the year before. Now that Sarah was in school for half of each day, Julia was taking a painting class and an art theory class. She hoped to one day complete the college art degree that she had abandoned so many years ago, and maybe go into teaching. She wasn't sure.

Jim was supportive in whatever she wanted to do. After Nicky's accident he made some decisions for himself and for their family. She could still clearly remember the emotional conversation in Nicky's hospital room when Jim had broken down and expressed such sorrow over the state of their marriage and told her how sick with worry he had been on the plane ride home from Chicago. The warmth and relief she felt when he tearfully vowed that he would never again put business over her or their children had been enough to carry her through that dangerously rough part of their marriage.

It wasn't always great, but they were both in it for the

long haul, for their kids, and for each other. Julia knew that life would have ups and downs, and she felt like she was in a better place to handle them now.

It was a beautiful day. She had about a thirty minute drive to the college, so she rolled down her window and turned up the radio. She didn't recognize the musical intro to the song that was playing, and started to dig through her purse with one hand to pull out her phone so she could listen to her own music. She stopped suddenly. The singer on the radio had started belting out the lyrics, and his voice was unmistakable.

> "Where are you now Love, where have you
>   been?
> Are you waiting for me in the eyes of a
>   friend..."

Julia couldn't believe it. Luckily, she came to a stoplight and stopped driving, because she was stunned and unable to think about anything but the sound floating through her car. It was Tyler...on the radio...and he was singing her song.

> "What have you done, love, why did you leave?
> Did you mean "no" Love, how can that be..."

Tyler's voice brought back his touch, his smile, his laugh, everything came flooding once again through Julia as she sat at the stoplight, tears in her eyes. The tears were unexplainable, really. They were sad, yes, but also joyful, and full of affection for him and everything that he meant to her.

There was nothing for her to do but to feel the sensations that moved through her body, and listen to his song as it wrapped around her soul. She listened with pleasure, with pain, and with love.

"I was alive once, now I am free,
I was afraid, Love, but you stayed with me..."

The driver of the car that sat behind her honked his horn. The light had turned green, she hadn't noticed. Julia wiped the tears from her cheeks, turned up the volume and drove on.

The End

ALSO BY DARCI BALOGH

ABOUT THE AUTHOR

Darci Balogh is a single mother turned filmmaker and author living in Denver, Colorado. She loves dogs, coffee, matinee movies, drinking wine on a patio in the sunshine and writing about rediscovering passion.

After divorcing in her late 30's, Ms. Balogh turned to her true passion in life...telling stories. She has a particular affinity for unconventional love stories because of her personal experiences. She believes that attraction has nothing to do with age or looks, and that love can happen anywhere...anytime...so be on the lookout!

To see other books by Darci Balogh,
as well as more great titles, go to
www.knowheremedia.com/books

www.ingramcontent.com/pod-product-compliance
Lightning Source LLC
Chambersburg PA
CBHW060441180626
46817CB00007B/2917